The Pittsburgh Steelers became the first team to win six Super Bowls.

trophies high. Go crazy with soccer players scoring big goals. And walk around a fan-filled ballpark carrying the World Series trophy.

Sports is about heroes, too, and they're all in here. Our star-studded cast includes Ryan Howard, Derek Jeter, Larry Fitzgerald, Santonio Holmes, Tim Tebow, Tyler Hansbrough, Maya Moore, Kobe Bryant, LeBron James, Sidney Crosby, Jimmie Johnson, Shaun White, Serena Williams, Marta, Kaka, Cristiano Ronaldo, Tiger Woods, Lorena Ochoa, Lance Armstrong, and many, many others. It's an action-packed ride through 363 days of sports!

So, what about those missing two days? Easy. The day before and the day after the Major League All-Star Game. Tell you what: In 2010, spend those days reading this book!

The Williams sisters have eight Wimbledon titles.

TOP 10 MOMENTS IN SPORTS

8•2008 ▸ 8•2009

How many of these memorable moments from the world of sports can you identify?

We're kicking off the *Scholastic Year in Sports* with a look at what we think were the top 10 moments or accomplishments of the past 12 months. You might not agree with all of our choices, but you'll surely agree that all of these athletes and teams made a huge mark on their parts of the sports world. (Plus, can you guess which was the number-one moment in the past year?)

After this, we break down all the top sports and give you the latest and greatest, the hottest and newest, and all the stats you need!

SCHOLASTIC

YEAR IN SPORTS 2010

SCHOLASTIC INC.

New York • Toronto • London • Auckland
Sydney • Mexico City • New Delhi • Hong Kong

ISBN-13: 978-0-545-16061-2
ISBN-10: 0-545-16061-8

10 9 8 7 6 5 4 3 2 09 10 11 12 13

Printed in the U.S.A. 40
First printing, December 2009

Produced by Shoreline Publishing Group LLC

Due to the publication date, records and statistics are current as of August 2009.

CONTENTS

INTRODUCTION

Did you know that there are only two days of the year on which there are zero games in at least one of the four major pro sports? Think about it, and we'll tell you what they are at the end of this introduction.

So that leaves 363 days (heck, 364 days in a leap year!) jam-packed with sports. And, of course, there's lots more to sports than just the four big pro leagues. College sports, smaller leagues, individual contests, races, matches, meets, events, tournaments, and on and on. If you're a sports nut, you can find something to entertain you on just about every day of the year. Because you probably can't see every sporting event you'd like to see, we're giving you this combination review and preview of a year in sports.

Inside, we'll take you through the pride and power of an NFL season; the ups and downs of the long NBA (and WNBA) grind; and the twists and turns (lots and lots of turns!) in NASCAR's year of racing. You'll sweat alongside tennis superstars, feel the tension of a clutch putt in golf. Ride alongside cyclists in the Tour de France, dive in the sand with beach volleyball stars, and go for "big air" with superstars on wheels at the X Games.

Sports is about winners, of course. Watch hockey's champions raise the Stanley Cup and see college hoops heroes hold their

The L.A. Lakers captured their 15th NBA championship.

7
6
5
4
3
2...

10 *Twenty-seven men up and twenty-seven men down: A perfect game is one of the rarest feats in baseball. In the summer of 2009, the Chicago White Sox's Mark Buehrle joined the elite group of 18 men who have been perfect.*

9 *First he promised . . . then he delivered. After an early-season loss, Florida QB Tim Tebow inspired his team and led them to the 2008 college football championship.*

8 That's Jimmie Johnson dancing in the smoky mist, celebrating his amazing third straight NASCAR championship. He was the second driver ever to "threepeat."

7 Japan won a real "world" series by capturing its second World Baseball Classic. Ichiro Suzuki held up the trophy after driving in the winning run in a thrilling final game.

6 *Usain Bolt has the right name for the "fastest man in the world." Jamaica's Bolt set yet another world record in the 100 meters—9.58 seconds in August 2009.*

5 *The Lakers became "Kobe's Team" the moment Shaquille O'Neal left. Kobe came through in 2009, leading "his" team to victory over Orlando in the NBA finals.*

4 *He's only topping himself at this point. After missing nearly a year following knee surgery, Tiger Woods roared back to the top with a win at Bay Hill.*

3

In one of horse racing's biggest upsets, 50–1 underdog Mine That Bird surprised everyone by winning the fabled Kentucky Derby.

2 *NOBODY saw this coming: The Tampa Bay Rays stunned the baseball world by capturing their first AL championship in a truly Cinderella fashion.*

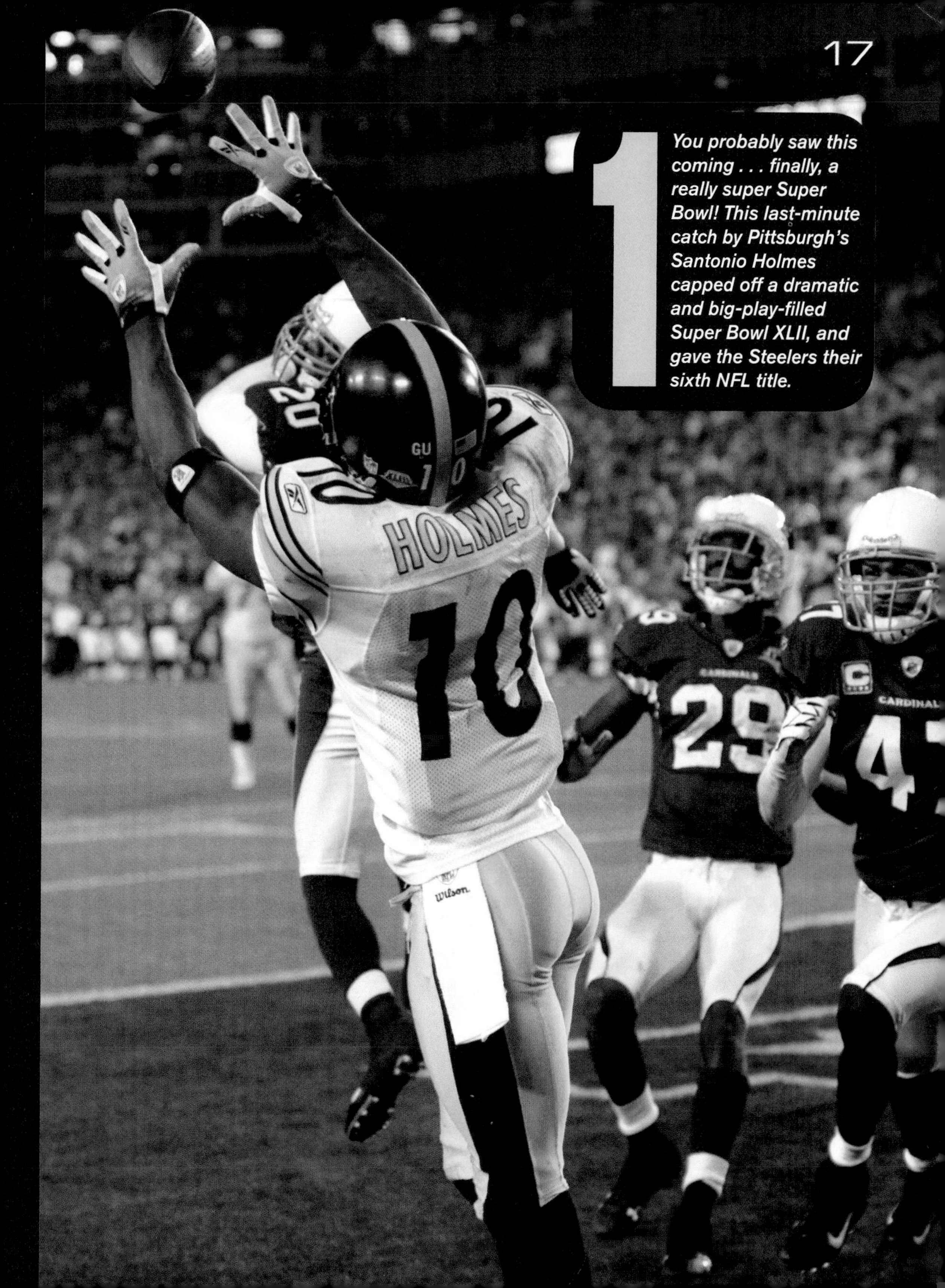

1 *You probably saw this coming . . . finally, a really super Super Bowl! This last-minute catch by Pittsburgh's Santonio Holmes capped off a dramatic and big-play-filled Super Bowl XLII, and gave the Steelers their sixth NFL title.*

JASON
FLIED OUT IN
AT BAT 8
1 2 3 4 5
RAYS 0 0 0 0 0
WHITE SOX 0 4 0 0 1
56

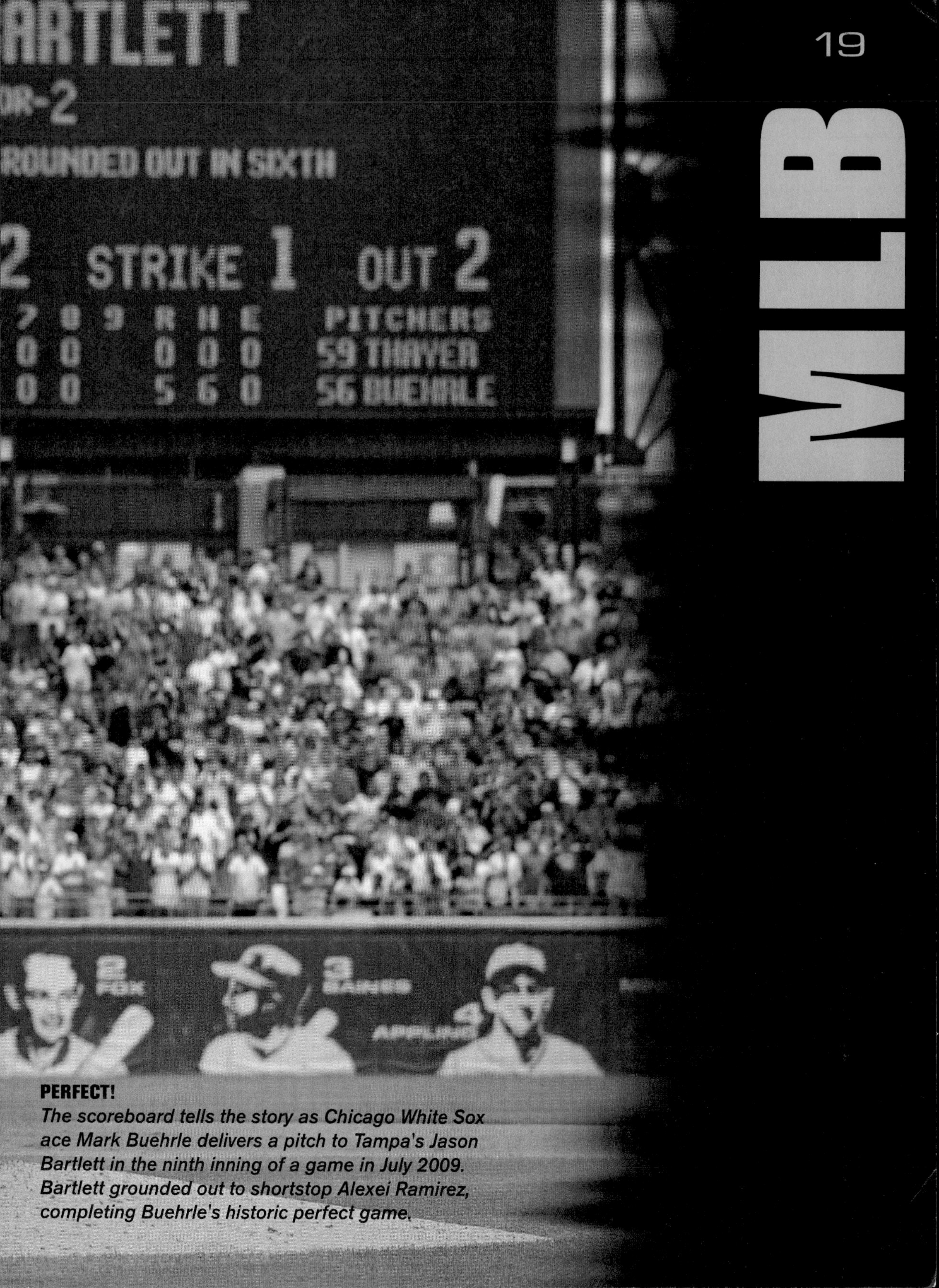

PERFECT!

The scoreboard tells the story as Chicago White Sox ace Mark Buehrle delivers a pitch to Tampa's Jason Bartlett in the ninth inning of a game in July 2009. Bartlett grounded out to shortstop Alexei Ramirez, completing Buehrle's historic perfect game.

UNEXPECTED HEROES

Dog pile! The jubilant Phillies won the '08 Series.

When the 2008 season began, no one thought the Tampa Bay Rays and Philadelphia Phillies would be fighting for the World Series trophy! The young Rays were regulars at the bottom of the AL East and had never made the play-offs. The Phillies had one World Series win since they were founded . . . in 1883! Yet as October headed into winter, the Phillies were in a dog pile and the Tampa Bay Rays enjoyed the respect of the baseball world for their stunning season.

Also, when the season began, no one expected that the Yankees would miss the play-offs. After all, they had been there every year since 1996. But in a year in which the team and the city said good-bye to the original Yankee Stadium (1923–2008), the Yankees said good-bye to their play-off hopes as the Rays and Red Sox kept them out.

An early-season 2008 highlight was a no-hitter pitched by Jon Lester of the Red Sox over the Royals. Just another no-hitter? Not quite. Just two years earlier, Lester was battling cancer. But he worked hard and came back to join one of baseball's best teams. Speaking of comebacks, Josh Hamilton, an outfielder with Texas, was putting on a stunning display of hitting. Once a top draft pick, Hamilton had sunk into drug use and trouble. With the help of family and friends, he returned to baseball and led the AL in RBI.

While the Rays and the Phils were the biggest news, other teams in the play-offs

THREE BIG MOVES Three important superstars changed uniforms during the 2008 season and all three of them led their new teams into the play-offs. Making a move like that can be risky, but daring paid off for the Dodgers, Angels, and Brewers.

The Dodgers got Boston superslugger Manny Ramirez in a three-team trade. Manny's bat was on fire in the late summer and fall, and the Dodgers won the NL West. Down the freeway in Anaheim, the Angels picked up first baseman Mark Teixeira for the play-off run and he helped them post the best record in the AL. In the Midwest, big C. C. Sabathia moved from Cleveland to Milwaukee. He was so good, he ended up leading both leagues in shutouts . . . in one season!

Jon Lester celebrates his no-hitter.

were surprises as well. The Brewers were there for the first time in 26 years (see box). The White Sox had to survive some extra games to earn a spot (see page 25). After the dust of the play-offs settled, though, the "expected" teams–the Red Sox and the Cubs–were at home watching TV, while the "surprise" teams headed for their World Series date.

"Now we're winners. Rejoice! No one can take this away from the city of Philadelphia!"

— RYAN HOWARD

The slippers came off the Cinderella Rays during the World Series, and the Phillies, led by pitcher Cole Hamels and slugger Ryan Howard, won the title.

The 2009 season might be marked with the bad news of Alex Rodriguez and Manny Ramirez off the field (see page 25), but on the field, new surprises and success stories (Mark Buehrle was perfect!) were cropping up all over the league.

2008 FINAL STANDINGS

AL EAST	
Rays	97-65
Red Sox	95-67
Yankees	89-73
Blue Jays	86-76
Orioles	69-83
AL CENTRAL	
White Sox	89-74
Twins	88-75
Indians	81-81
Royals	75-87
Tigers	74-88
AL WEST	
Angels	100-62
Rangers	79-83
Athletics	75-86
Mariners	61-101
NL EAST	
Phillies	92-70
Mets	89-73
Marlins	84-77
Braves	72-90
Nationals	59-102
NL CENTRAL	
Cubs	97-64
Brewers	90-72
Astros	86-75
Cardinals	86-76
Reds	74-88
Pirates	67-95
NL WEST	
Dodgers	84-78
Diamondbacks	82-80
Rockies	74-88
Giants	72-90
Padres	63-99

THE BEST OF THE BEST

Here's a look at the key 2008 award winners for baseball.

MOST VALUABLE PLAYER

AL: **Dustin PEDROIA,** ▸▸▸
BOSTON RED SOX

NL: **Albert PUJOLS,**
ST. LOUIS CARDINALS

CY YOUNG AWARD

AL: **Cliff LEE,**
CLEVELAND INDIANS

NL: **Tim LINCECUM,**
SAN FRANCISCO GIANTS

ROOKIE OF THE YEAR

AL: **Evan LONGORIA,**
TAMPA BAY RAYS

NL: **Geovany SOTO,**
CHICAGO CUBS

RELIEF PITCHER OF THE YEAR

AL: **Francisco RODRIGUEZ,**
LOS ANGELES ANGELS

NL: **Brad LIDGE,**
PHILADELPHIA PHILLIES

MANAGER OF THE YEAR

AL: **Joe MADDON,**
TAMPA BAY RAYS

NL: **Lou PINIELLA,**
CHICAGO CUBS

HANK AARON AWARD

(Voted by fans as the top offensive performers in each league)

Kevin YOUKILIS,
BOSTON RED SOX

Aramis RAMIREZ,
CHICAGO CUBS

ROBERTO CLEMENTE AWARD

(Given by Major League Baseball to honor a player's work in the community)

Albert PUJOLS,
ST. LOUIS CARDINALS

By the Numbers

AL HITTING LEADERS

HOME RUNS: 37
Miguel CABRERA, TIGERS

RBI: 130
Josh HAMILTON, RANGERS

AVERAGE: .328
Joe MAUER, TWINS

STOLEN BASES: 50
Jacoby ELLSBURY, RED SOX

HITS: 213
Dustin PEDROIA, RED SOX,
Ichiro SUZUKI, MARINERS

NL HITTING LEADERS

HOME RUNS: 48
Ryan HOWARD, PHILLIES

RBI: 146
Ryan HOWARD, PHILLIES

AVERAGE: .364
Chipper JONES, BRAVES

STOLEN BASES: 68
Willy TAVERAS, ROCKIES

HITS: 204
Jose REYES, METS

AL PITCHING LEADERS

WINS: 22 **Cliff LEE,** INDIANS ▶▶▶

SAVES: 62
Francisco RODRIGUEZ, ANGELS

ERA: 2.54 **Cliff LEE,** INDIANS

STRIKEOUTS: 231
A. J. BURNETT, BLUE JAYS

INNINGS: 248
Roy HALLADAY, BLUE JAYS

NL PITCHING LEADERS

WINS: 22
Brandon WEBB, DIAMONDBACKS

SAVES: 44
Jose VALVERDE, ASTROS

ERA: 2.53
Johan SANTANA, METS

STRIKEOUTS: 265
Tim LINCECUM, GIANTS

INNINGS: 234.1
Johan SANTANA, METS

AROUND THE BASES

Bobblehead Bonus
Hometown fans at a July 2009 game in Los Angeles between the Dodgers and the Cincinnati Reds were delighted to receive Manny Ramirez bobblehead figures when they walked through the gates. They got an extra gift when the injured Ramirez came off the bench in the sixth inning to belt a tie-breaking, grand-slam home run, lifting the Dodgers to a 6–2 victory.

WISE MOVE
On July 23, 2009, the Chicago White Sox's Mark Buehrle pitched only the 18th perfect game in big-league history when he blanked the Tampa Rays 5–0 (see the photo on pages 18–19). Buehrle's gem was saved when center fielder DeWayne Wise made an unforgettable catch to keep Tampa's Gabe Kapler from scoring in the ninth inning. Wise had just been inserted into the game by White Sox manager Ozzie Guillen for defensive purposes.

All-Star Catch
In the seventh inning of the 2009 All-Star Game in St. Louis, Tampa's Carl Crawford reached up over the left-field wall to take a home run away from Colorado's Brad Hawpe and preserve a 3–3 tie. The American League scored a run the next inning and went on to win 4–3, running its unbeaten string in the Midsummer Classic to 13 years. Crawford went 1-for-3 at the plate, but his big play on D earned him game MVP honors, making him the first player ever to win the award without scoring or driving in a run.

Giant Gem
San Francisco left-hander Jonathan Sanchez tossed the first no-hitter of the 2009 season when he beat the San Diego Padres 8–0 on July 10. It was the first no-hitter by a Giants pitcher in 33 years.

Oops!
White Sox outfielder Carlos Quentin was probably going to be the 2008 AL MVP until he slammed his hand into his bat after striking out in a September game. He broke his wrist and had to miss the rest of the season.

Still Playing!
It took the White Sox some extra work to earn the AL Central title for the 2008 season. First they had to win the makeup of an earlier rained-out game, and then a tiebreaker play-off game over the Twins. Unfortunately for Chicago fans, the Tampa Bay Rays cleaned up the Sox in the Division Series.

Good-bye to Old Friends

The 2008 season was the last for the original Yankee Stadium. "The House That Ruth Built" (that would be Babe Ruth, of course) was closed to make way for a brand-new Yankee Stadium that opened in April 2009. New York's other team got a new stadium in 2009, too. The Mets tore down Shea Stadium and moved into Citi Field.

Reliever Mariano Rivera collected dirt from the Yankee Stadium mound.

No DH in the AL?

Thanks to a mistake by Rays manager Joe Maddon, pitcher Andy Sonnanstine hit third in a game in May 2009. Maddon listed two third basemen and no designated hitter. The umps made him take out 3B Evan Longoria and put in Sonnanstine–the first AL pitcher since 1976 to be in the batting order.

BAD BOYS

Two of baseball's greatest all-time stars admitted using drugs that were against baseball's rules. After it was revealed in early 2009 that he had tested positive for steroids, Alex Rodriguez (right) admitted using such drugs during his years with the Texas Rangers. He said he had stopped after 2003, but it was a black mark against one of the game's greatest talents. The baseball world was still reeling from that when it was revealed in May 2009 that Manny Ramirez (left) was suspended for 50 games. He admitted to using a type of drug that was against baseball's rules. This double dose of bad choices by players who were so well liked and so talented made many fans continue to question who else was cheating.

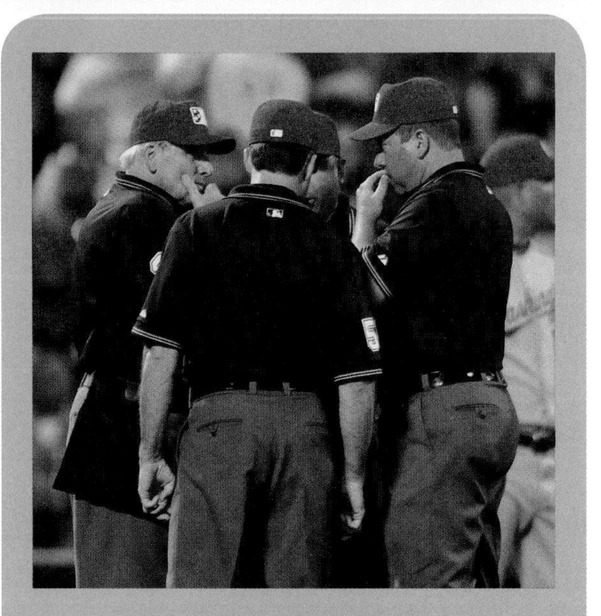

PLAY IT AGAIN (ON TAPE)

Instant replay was used for the first time in Major League Baseball in 2008. Umpires could check TV monitors to see replays of home run calls, fan interference, and other situations. It was only used occasionally, but some calls were reversed after "going to the tape."

THREE IN ONE!

Baseball's rarest defensive event is the unassisted triple play. That means one player records all three outs on one batted ball. It happened again on August 23, 2009, when Philly's Eric Bruntlett, playing second base, caught a line drive, stepped on second to force one runner, and made the third out by tagging the runner coming from first. Best part? It ended the game and gave the Phillies a win over the rival Mets! It was only the second of the 15 such plays to end a game.

JETER TOPS GEHRIG

It's not every day that a record that has stood for 70 years falls, but that's what happened in September 2009. Yankees shortstop Derek Jeter set a new all-time record for hits by a Yankee. His single against Baltimore topped the old record of 2,712 set by the great Lou "The Iron Horse" Gehrig, who last played in 1939.

THE LAST 300?

In June, Randy Johnson earned his 300th career win. He became the 24th pitcher to reach this illustrious mark. The mighty lefty led the Giants to a 5–1 victory over the Nationals. Already second all-time in strikeouts, Johnson is a surefire Hall of Famer one day. He might also be the last pitcher to reach 300 wins. The only other active pitcher within 50 wins of 300 is Jamie Moyer (and he's 46). In fact, only four active pitchers, all 37 or older, have even 200 wins! So, way to go, Big Unit!

BROKEN RECORDS

HIGHEST ATTENDANCE

115,300 RED SOX at Dodgers The 2008 preseason game held at the Los Angeles Memorial Coliseum was a massive sellout and broke a record set in 1959, also at the Coliseum.

◀◀◀ SAVES IN A SEASON

62 FRANCISO RODRIGUEZ, Angels The old record was 57, set in 1990 by Bobby Thigpen of the White Sox.

SCORELESS INNINGS TO START A CAREER

39 BRAD ZIEGLER, Athletics The sidearm hurler baffled hitters and got his career off to a very hot start. The old record was 22 innings!

CYCLES IN ONE DAY

2 STEPHEN DREW, Arizona, ADRIAN BELTRE, Seattle
The last time two players hit for the cycle on the same day was in 1920!

MOST STRIKEOUTS BY A BATTER

204 MARK REYNOLDS, Arizona ▶▶▶ That's pretty bad, but then again, the old record was held by 2008 NL MVP Ryan Howard with 199.

MOST GAMES IN A ROW WITHOUT AN ERROR (BY A TEAM)

18 NEW YORK YANKEES The Bronx Bombers flashed the leather as they set a new mark for "perfect" games . . . fielding-wise, that is, during a May–June stretch in 2009.

2008 POSTSEASON

AL DIVISION SERIES

Red Sox 3, Angels 1
After the Angels won a 12-inning battle to stay alive, a blown squeeze bunt in Game 4 opened the door for the Sox to clinch the series.

Rays 3, White Sox 1
The Rays' great starting pitching closed down Chicago's strong offense.

L.A. closer Jonathon Broxton celebrates.

NL DIVISION SERIES

Phillies 3, Brewers 1
Milwaukee's miracle run ended when they managed only 15 total hits in their three losses to Philly.

Dodgers 3, Cubs 0
This series saw a stunning sweep of the NL's best team by a Dodgers club that had won only one play-off game since 1988.

AL CHAMPIONSHIP SERIES

Rays 4, Red Sox 3
After Daisuke Matsuzaka nearly no-hit Tampa Bay to win Game 1, the Rays' bats woke up. They scored 9, 9, and 13 runs in winning three straight. However, in Game 5, the Red Sox pulled off the biggest postseason rally in 80 years. Down by seven with seven outs to go, they ended up winning 8–7 on a walk-off single by J. D. Drew. After Boston stayed alive again with a Game 6 win, the Rays' masterful pitching carried them to the AL title with a 3–1 Game 7 win.

NL CHAMPIONSHIP SERIES

Phillies 4, Dodgers 1
Even though Manny Ramirez cracked a pair of homers for L.A., Philly won the first two games. The Dodgers came back to win Game 5, but Cole Hamels shut them down to clinch the Phillies' first trip to the World Series since 1983.

2008 WORLD SERIES: THE TWO-

GAME 1

Phillies 3—Rays 2

Starting pitcher Cole Hamels, the eventual Series MVP, joined with the Phillies' bull pen to shut down the Rays' powerful bats.

WP: *Cole Hamels;* **LP:** *Scott Kazmir*
HR: *Phil: Chase Utley; TB: Carl Crawford*

GAME 2

Rays 4—Phillies 2

Not the prettiest game, but a win's a win. James Shields was solid while the Phillies moved to 1-for-28 with runners in scoring position in two Series games. Rookie David Price was also a pitching star, striking out Ryan Howard in the seventh and then closing out the win.

WP: *James Shields;* **LP:** *Randy Myers*
HR: *Phil: Eric Bruntlett*

GAME 3

Phillies 5—Rays 4

A game that started more than two hours late due to a rainstorm ended up after midnight on a bases-loaded dribbler against a five-man infield! After Tampa tied the game 4–4 in the eighth inning, Philly loaded the bases in the ninth on a hit batter, a wild pitch, a throwing error, and two intentional walks. Carlos Ruiz hit a ball that just squirted far enough out to score the winning run.

WP: *J. C. Romero;* **LP:** *Jay Howell*
HR: *Phil: Carlos Ruiz, Chase Utley, Ryan Howard*

Ryan Howard holds the World Series trophy; Cole Hamels grabbed the Series MVP.

GAME 4

Phillies 10—Rays 2

Ryan Howard socked two homers. Philly's Joe Blanton hit the first Series HR by a pitcher in 34 years.

WP: *Joe Blanton;* **LP:** *Andy Sonnanstine*
HR: *Phil: Ryan Howard (2), Joe Blanton, Jayson Werth;* **TB:** *Carl Crawford*

GAME 5

Phillies 4—Rays 3

A weird ending to a weird season. Tied 2–2 in the bottom of the sixth, a driving rainstorm suspended the game. Two days later, the game continued . . . for three innings! Philly scored twice and closer Brad Lidge hung tough. An amazing ending!

WP: *J. C. Romero;* **LP:** *Jay Howell*
HR: **TB:** *Baldelli*

WORLD SERIES MVP: **P COLE HAMELS**, Philadelphia – 13 IP, 10 hits, 3 BB, 8 Ks, 1-0, 2.77

TOMORROW'S LEGENDS TODAY

Who will be a star at the level of Cardinals stud Albert Pujols in five years? What pitchers will hitters still fear in 2015? Here are some young superstars on the rise in 2009 and 2010.

Ryan BRAUN, OF, MILWAUKEE

He's not exactly news anymore, not after a pair of 30-homer seasons, but Braun is a great combination of power and hitting skill.

Evan LONGORIA, 3B, TAMPA

The 2008 AL Rookie of the Year has a powerful bat and is already one of the best-fielding third basemen in recent history.

◀◀◀ Zack GREINKE, P, KANSAS CITY

After scrabbling for a couple of seasons, he came into his own in 2009, getting off to one of the hottest starts in years. It says here he'll keep it going.

Carlos QUENTIN, OF, CHICAGO

If he hadn't broken his hand (see page 24), Carlos might have been MVP. As it is, he's still the best young power hitter in the AL.

Joey VOTTO, 1B, CINCINNATI

Second in the 2008 Rookie of the Year race, this Canadian slugger might help kick-start another Big Red Machine.

2010 Preview

Why wait? Here's a look at some youngsters who might make a mark in 2010.

Madison BUMGARNER, P, SAN FRANCISCO: Another lively arm to help Cy Young star Tim Lincecum

Jason HEYWARD, OF, ATLANTA: All-around skills, but still only 19

Matt LaPORTA, OF, CLEVELAND: Some are calling him a future All-Star regular

David PRICE, P, TAMPA BAY: Already has play-off experience and could join Tampa Bay full-time as a starter or closer

Colby RASMUS, OF, ST. LOUIS: Solid hitter, could help the Cards very soon

Justin SMOAK, 1B, TEXAS: A switch-hitter with big power, Smoak could make a strong Rangers lineup even stronger

Stephen STRASBURG, P, WASHINGTON: Topped 100 mph in college as well as the 2009 draft; might be a year away, but his talents have coaches drooling

Matt WIETERS, C, BALTIMORE: Big, switch-hitting bat could end up at DH

LITTLE BIG MEN

Teams from around the world travel to Williamsport, PA, each summer for the Little League World Series (LLWS). The 2008 winner was from the United States, but still had to travel farther than the team it beat! That's because the champion was from Waipio Little League on the island of Oahu in Hawaii. They beat a team from Matamoros, Mexico, 12–3 in the final. In 2009, the U.S. made it two in a row. The team from Chula Vista, CA, near San Diego, came from behind to defeat the team from Taiwan. Chula Vista had slugged 19 homers in the LLWS before the final game, but they won that last game without a long ball.

Chula Vista's Nick Conlin slides in to score a tying run on a wild pitch in the 2009 LLWS championship game.

WORLD BASEBALL CLASSIC

The 2009 edition of this international baseball competition was a huge hit. Top players from the Major Leagues and other pro organizations represented their countries in March 2009. The final four were the United States, Venezuela, Korea, and Japan. Korea and Japan met in the final game.

After both teams paraded onto the field accompanied by drum groups from their homelands, they put on a great display of baseball. Superb pitching, great defense, timely hitting . . . all as fans from both teams filled the air with chants, noise, and cheering. It went to extra innings after Korea tied the score 3–3 with a run in the bottom of the ninth. In the 10th inning, Japan got runners to second and third. That brought up superstar Ichiro Suzuki. He proved why he was one of the best hitters in the world by delivering a single that ended up giving Japan its second straight WBC championship.

> ***“I knew everyone in Japan was focused on me. So I was just happy that I could get the hit we needed.”***
>
> **— ICHIRO SUZUKI**

RICKEY AND RICE

Cooperstown, New York, has new residents. In August 2009, the Baseball Hall of Fame welcomed two famous new members: outfielders Rickey Henderson (right) and Jim Rice. Henderson, who played for nine teams, got in on his first try, which was no surprise since he's the all-time leader in runs and stolen bases. He's also probably the best leadoff hitter in baseball history. Rice took longer to get there, earning election on his 15th try. The slugger was the 1978 AL MVP and was a feared power hitter for more than a decade with Boston. Former Yankees second baseman Joe Gordon was also chosen for the Hall by the Veterans' Committee.

2009 WORLD SERIES: A PREDICTION

Well, we had to print this book before the 2009 World Series happened. So we can't tell you who won . . . but we can guess. Based on our vast knowledge of baseball, what we've seen in 2009, and what our crystal baseball is showing, we predict that the 2009 World Series champion will be (envelope, please):

★St. Louis Cardinals★

WORLD SERIES WINNERS

YEAR	WINNER	RUNNER-UP	SCORE*
2008	Philadelphia Phillies	Tampa Bay Rays	4-1
2007	Boston Red Sox	Colorado Rockies	4-0
2006	St. Louis Cardinals	Detroit Tigers	4-1
2005	Chicago White Sox	Houston Astros	4-0
2004	Boston Red Sox	St. Louis Cardinals	4-0
2003	Florida Marlins	New York Yankees	4-2
2002	Anaheim Angels	San Francisco Giants	4-3
2001	Arizona Diamondbacks	New York Yankees	4-3
2000	New York Yankees	New York Mets	4-1
1999	New York Yankees	Atlanta Braves	4-0
1998	New York Yankees	San Diego Padres	4-0
1997	Florida Marlins	Cleveland Indians	4-3
1996	New York Yankees	Atlanta Braves	4-2
1995	Atlanta Braves	Cleveland Indians	4-2
1993	Toronto Blue Jays	Philadelphia Phillies	4-2
1992	Toronto Blue Jays	Atlanta Braves	4-2
1991	Minnesota Twins	Atlanta Braves	4-3
1990	Cincinnati Reds	Oakland Athletics	4-0
1989	Oakland Athletics	San Francisco Giants	4-0
1988	Los Angeles Dodgers	Oakland Athletics	4-1
1987	Minnesota Twins	St. Louis Cardinals	4-3
1986	New York Mets	Boston Red Sox	4-3
1985	Kansas City Royals	St. Louis Cardinals	4-3
1984	Detroit Tigers	San Diego Padres	4-1

YEAR	WINNER	RUNNER-UP	SCORE*
1983	Baltimore Orioles	Philadelphia Phillies	4-1
1982	St. Louis Cardinals	Milwaukee Brewers	4-3
1981	Los Angeles Dodgers	New York Yankees	4-2
1980	Philadelphia Phillies	Kansas City Royals	4-2
1979	Pittsburgh Pirates	Baltimore Orioles	4-3
1978	New York Yankees	Los Angeles Dodgers	4-2
1977	New York Yankees	Los Angeles Dodgers	4-2
1976	Cincinnati Reds	New York Yankees	4-0
1975	Cincinnati Reds	Boston Red Sox	4-3
1974	Oakland Athletics	Los Angeles Dodgers	4-1
1973	Oakland Athletics	New York Mets	4-3
1972	Oakland Athletics	Cincinnati Reds	4-3
1971	Pittsburgh Pirates	Baltimore Orioles	4-3
1970	Baltimore Orioles	Cincinnati Reds	4-1
1969	New York Mets	Baltimore Orioles	4-1
1968	Detroit Tigers	St. Louis Cardinals	4-3
1967	St. Louis Cardinals	Boston Red Sox	4-3
1966	Baltimore Orioles	Los Angeles Dodgers	4-0
1965	Los Angeles Dodgers	Minnesota Twins	4-3
1964	St. Louis Cardinals	New York Yankees	4-3
1963	Los Angeles Dodgers	New York Yankees	4-0
1962	New York Yankees	San Francisco Giants	4-3
1961	New York Yankees	Cincinnati Reds	4-1
1960	Pittsburgh Pirates	New York Yankees	4-3

YEAR	WINNER	RUNNER-UP	SCORE*
1959	Los Angeles Dodgers	Chicago White Sox	4-2
1958	New York Yankees	Milwaukee Braves	4-3
1957	Milwaukee Braves	New York Yankees	4-3
1956	New York Yankees	Brooklyn Dodgers	4-3
1955	Brooklyn Dodgers	New York Yankees	4-3
1954	New York Giants	Cleveland Indians	4-0
1953	New York Yankees	Brooklyn Dodgers	4-2
1952	New York Yankees	Brooklyn Dodgers	4-3
1951	New York Yankees	New York Giants	4-2
1950	New York Yankees	Philadelphia Phillies	4-0
1949	New York Yankees	Brooklyn Dodgers	4-1
1948	Cleveland Indians	Boston Braves	4-2
1947	New York Yankees	Brooklyn Dodgers	4-3
1946	St. Louis Cardinals	Boston Red Sox	4-3
1945	Detroit Tigers	Chicago Cubs	4-3
1944	St. Louis Cardinals	St. Louis Browns	4-2
1943	New York Yankees	St. Louis Cardinals	4-1
1942	St. Louis Cardinals	New York Yankees	4-1
1941	New York Yankees	Brooklyn Dodgers	4-1
1940	Cincinnati Reds	Detroit Tigers	4-3
1939	New York Yankees	Cincinnati Reds	4-0
1938	New York Yankees	Chicago Cubs	4-0
1937	New York Yankees	New York Giants	4-1
1936	New York Yankees	New York Giants	4-2
1935	Detroit Tigers	Chicago Cubs	4-2
1934	St. Louis Cardinals	Detroit Tigers	4-3
1933	New York Giants	Washington Senators	4-1
1932	New York Yankees	Chicago Cubs	4-0

YEAR	WINNER	RUNNER-UP	SCORE*
1931	St. Louis Cardinals	Philadelphia Athletics	4-3
1930	Philadelphia Athletics	St. Louis Cardinals	4-2
1929	Philadelphia Athletics	Chicago Cubs	4-1
1928	New York Yankees	St. Louis Cardinals	4-0
1927	New York Yankees	Pittsburgh Pirates	4-0
1926	St. Louis Cardinals	New York Yankees	4-3
1925	Pittsburgh Pirates	Washington Senators	4-3
1924	Washington Senators	New York Giants	4-3
1923	New York Yankees	New York Giants	4-2
1922	New York Giants	New York Yankees	4-0
1921	New York Giants	New York Yankees	5-3
1920	Cleveland Indians	Brooklyn Dodgers	5-2
1919	Cincinnati Reds	Chicago White Sox	5-3
1918	Boston Red Sox	Chicago Cubs	4-2
1917	Chicago White Sox	New York Giants	4-2
1916	Boston Red Sox	Brooklyn Dodgers	4-1
1915	Boston Red Sox	Philadelphia Phillies	4-1
1914	Boston Braves	Philadelphia Athletics	4-0
1913	Philadelphia Athletics	New York Giants	4-1
1912	Boston Red Sox	New York Giants	4-3
1911	Philadelphia Athletics	New York Giants	4-2
1910	Philadelphia Athletics	Chicago Cubs	4-1
1909	Pittsburgh Pirates	Detroit Tigers	4-3
1908	Chicago Cubs	Detroit Tigers	4-1
1907	Chicago Cubs	Detroit Tigers	4-0
1906	Chicago White Sox	Chicago Cubs	4-2
1905	New York Giants	Philadelphia Athletics	4-1
1903	Boston Red Sox	Pittsburgh Pirates	5-3

* Score is represented in games played.

SUPER PLAY!
Pittsburgh linebacker James Harrison rumbles toward the end zone following an interception late in the second quarter of Super Bowl XLIII against Arizona in February of 2009. Harrison finished off his record 100-yard return in the Steelers' 27–23 victory.

92
CARDINALS
74
34

SEASON IN REVIEW

When Santonio Holmes latched on to a touchdown pass from Ben Roethlisberger in the final minute to give Pittsburgh a victory over Arizona in Super Bowl XLIII in February of 2009, he put an exclamation point on one of the most exciting NFL seasons in recent memory.

Holmes's catch gave the Steelers their record sixth Super Bowl victory. It also overshadowed a brilliant comeback spearheaded by Cardinals wide receiver Larry Fitzgerald. His 64-yard catch just a few minutes before Holmes's grab capped an amazing stretch of games for him. In the Cardinals' four postseason games, Fitzgerald caught 30 passes for 546 yards and 7 touchdowns. Add on 96 catches in the regular season, and Fitzgerald took over as the NFL's best pass catcher.

Fitzgerald left all other WRs behind.

The best runner and the best passer were new in 2008, too. In only his second NFL season, Minnesota's Adrian Peterson won his first league rushing title. He gained 1,760 yards and helped lead the Vikings to a division title. New Orleans's Drew Brees passed for 5,069 yards and 34 touchdowns, but they weren't enough to get the Saints into the play-offs.

Among the teams that did make the play-offs, none was a bigger surprise than the Dolphins. Miami, which was 1–15 in 2007, went 11–5 in 2008 and won the AFC East under new coach Tony Sparano.

Two other teams reached the play-offs under rookie head coaches: Atlanta in the NFC and Baltimore in the AFC. Coach Mike Smith's Falcons and John Harbaugh's Ravens even did it with rookie QBs (Matt Ryan started for Atlanta, and Joe Flacco lined up for Baltimore).

Several rookie runners made their mark, too, like Houston's Steve Slaton (1,282 yards), Chicago's Matt Forté (1,238), and Tennessee's Chris Johnson (1,228).

It wasn't all about the rookies, though. Veteran quarterback Peyton Manning passed for more than 4,000 yards (he had 4,002) and was the NFL MVP. He succeeded Tom Brady, who never got a chance to build on his 2007 MVP season because he was injured in Week 1 and did not return until 2009.

As usual, though, nothing could keep quarterback Brett Favre out of the lineup—not even changing teams. After retiring at the end of the 2007 season, Favre came back and was traded from Green Bay to the New York Jets. By season's end, Favre had extended his own NFL-record streak to 269 consecutive starts. He also passed for 3,472 yards and 22 touchdowns. In 2009, he joined the Minnesota Vikings (page 48).

If all of those stats sound like there was a whole lot of offense going on, it's because there was. NFL teams combined to average 44.1 points per game in 2008. That was the highest total in 43 years.

Manning: 4,000 yards for ninth time.

Final 2008 Regular-Season Standings

AFC EAST	W	L	T
Miami	11	5	0
New England	11	5	0
N.Y. Jets	9	7	0
Buffalo	7	9	0

AFC NORTH	W	L	T
Pittsburgh	12	4	0
Baltimore	11	5	0
Cincinnati	4	11	1
Cleveland	4	12	0

AFC SOUTH	W	L	T
Tennessee	13	3	0
Indianapolis	12	4	0
Houston	8	8	0
Jacksonville	5	11	0

AFC WEST	W	L	T
San Diego	8	8	0
Denver	8	8	0
Oakland	5	11	0
Kansas City	2	14	0

NFC EAST	W	L	T
N.Y. Giants	12	4	0
Philadelphia	9	6	1
Dallas	9	7	0
Washington	8	8	0

NFC NORTH	W	L	T
Minnesota	10	6	0
Chicago	9	7	0
Green Bay	6	10	0
Detroit	0	16	0

NFC SOUTH	W	L	T
Carolina	12	4	0
Atlanta	11	5	0
Tampa Bay	9	7	0
New Orleans	8	8	0

NFC WEST	W	L	T
Arizona	9	7	0
San Francisco	7	9	0
Seattle	4	12	0
St. Louis	2	14	0

THE 2008 POSTSEASON

Here's how the road to Super Bowl XLIII went. (Home teams are listed in caps.)

Darren Sproles' TD lifted San Diego over the Colts.

Wild-Card Weekend

AFC Baltimore 27, **MIAMI** 9
SAN DIEGO 23, Indianapolis 17 (OT)

NFC Philadelphia 26, **MINNESOTA** 14
ARIZONA 30, Atlanta 24

Divisional Play-offs

AFC **PITTSBURGH** 35, San Diego 24
Baltimore 13, **TENNESSEE** 10

NFC Philadelphia 23, **N.Y. GIANTS** 11
Arizona 33, **CAROLINA** 13

Conference Championships

AFC **PITTSBURGH** 23, Baltimore 14
NFC **ARIZONA** 32, Philadelphia 25

Super Bowl XLIII

Pittsburgh 27, Arizona 23

MVP Colts quarterback Peyton Manning is more than the guy you see on a bunch of funny television commercials. He's a pretty good football player, too! Manning passed for 4,002 yards and 27 TDs in 2008 to earn NFL MVP honors from the Associated Press for the third time. (Brett Favre is the only other player to win it three times.)

Manning's performance was even more impressive because he got off to a slow start following off-season knee surgery. He rebounded to lead the Colts to the play-offs for the seventh year in a row.

Best of the Best

These players were named by the Associated Press as first-team All-Pros for 2008:

OFFENSE

QUARTERBACK: **Peyton MANNING,** Indianapolis

RUNNING BACKS: **Adrian PETERSON,** Minnesota; **Michael TURNER,** Atlanta

FULLBACK: **Le'Ron McCLAIN,** Baltimore

TIGHT END: **Tony GONZALEZ,** Kansas City

WIDE RECEIVERS: **Andre JOHNSON,** Houston; **Larry FITZGERALD,** Arizona

TACKLES: **Jordan GROSS,** Carolina; **Michael ROOS,** Tennessee

GUARDS: **Steve HUTCHINSON,** Minnesota; **Chris SNEE,** N.Y. Giants

CENTER: **Kevin MAWAE,** Tennessee

KICKER: **Stephen GOSTKOWSKI,** New England

KICK RETURNER: **Leon WASHINGTON,** N.Y. Jets

DEFENSE

ENDS: **Justin TUCK,** N.Y. Giants; **Jared ALLEN,** Minnesota

TACKLES: **Albert HAYNESWORTH,** Tennessee; **Kevin WILLIAMS,** Minnesota

OUTSIDE LINEBACKERS: **DeMarcus WARE,** Dallas; **James HARRISON,** Pittsburgh

INSIDE LINEBACKERS: **Ray LEWIS,** Baltimore; **Jon BEASON,** Carolina

CORNERBACKS: **Nnamdi ASOMUGHA,** Oakland; **Cortland FINNEGAN,** Tennessee

SAFETIES: **Ed REED,** Baltimore; **Troy POLAMALU,** Pittsburgh

PUNTER: **Shane LECHLER,** Oakland

THE LEADERS

The top performers in some key NFL statistical categories for 2008:

DeAngelo Williams was a TD machine.

CATEGORY	PLAYER, TEAM	MARK
RUSHING	**Adrian Peterson,** Minnesota	1,760 yds.
PASSING	**Philip Rivers,** San Diego	105.5 rating
RECEIVING	**Andre Johnson,** Houston	115 catches
SCORING	**Stephen Gostkowski,** New England	148 pts.
TOUCHDOWNS	**DeAngelo Williams,** Carolina	20 TDs
SACKS	**DeMarcus Ware,** Dallas	20 sacks
INTERCEPTIONS	**Ed Reed,** Baltimore	9 ints.
FIELD GOALS	**Stephen Gostkowski,** New England	36 FGs
PUNTING	**Donnie Jones,** St. Louis	50.0 yards

TRIVIA

1 **BRETT FAVRE** retired—temporarily—after playing for the New York Jets in his 18th NFL season in 2008. Before that, Favre had been the quarterback of the Green Bay Packers. But what NFL team originally drafted Favre in the second round in 1991 before trading him to Green Bay the following season?

2 Baltimore safety **ED REED** set an NFL record when he returned an interception 107 yards for a touchdown against the Eagles in 2008. What player had held the longest return in league history at 106 yards?

3 **BERNARD BERRIAN'S** 99-yard touchdown catch for the Vikings in a game against the Bears in 2008 marked the 11th time in NFL history that a pass play covered that distance. Only one player, though, ever rushed 99 yards for a touchdown. Who was he?

Answers: 1. The Atlanta Falcons. 2. Ed Reed. He had a 106-yard return against the Browns in 2004. 3. Dallas's Tony Dorsett. His big run came against Minnesota in the 1982 season.

These players set NFL records or reached key milestones in 2008:

Drew Brees, QB, New Orleans
With 5,069 yards passing, he became only the second player in NFL history to reach 5,000 in a season. (Pro Football Hall of Fame quarterback Dan Marino holds the record with 5,084 yards for Miami in 1984.)

Isaac Bruce, WR, San Francisco
He joined the 49ers after 14 seasons with the rival Rams, and became just the fifth player to catch 1,000 passes in his career.

Brett Favre, QB, N.Y. Jets
Closed the season with an NFL-record 169 victories as a starting quarterback.

Larry Fitzgerald, WR, Arizona
Set a league record by catching 30 passes in a single postseason.

Tony Gonzalez, TE, Kansas City
Became the first tight end in NFL history to catch 900 passes.

Jason Hanson, K, Detroit
Set an NFL record with 41 career field goals of 50 or more yards.

Peyton Manning, QB, Indianapolis
Set NFL records with his ninth 4,000-yard passing season and his 11th consecutive season with 25 or more touchdown passes.

◀◀◀**Ed Reed,** S, Baltimore
Returned an interception against Philadelphia in an NFL-record 107 yards for a touchdown.

Matt Stover, K, Baltimore
Set an NFL record with 372 consecutive extra points made.

DeMarcus Ware, LB, Dallas
Equaled a league record by posting a sack in 10 consecutive games.

10 GREAT GAMES

The hardest thing about picking great games from an action-packed 2008 season is limiting the list to 10! If only we had more space. . . .

1 PITTSBURGH 27, Arizona 23 (Super Bowl XLIII)

Of course! One of the greatest Super Bowls ever capped a memorable season. The Steelers won it when Santonio Holmes made his big catch in the back corner of the end zone in the final minute. (See page 46 for more details.)

2 SAN DIEGO 23, Indianapolis 17 (AFC Wild-Card round, overtime)

With superstar LaDainian Tomlinson sidelined by an injury, backup Darren Sproles got his chance to shine. Sproles gained 328 combined net yards (rushing, receiving, and returns), the third most ever in an NFL postseason game. The last 22—on the game-winning run in OT—were the most important.

3 DENVER 39, San Diego 38 (Week 2)

The Chargers overcame a 17-point halftime deficit to take a 38–31 advantage late in the fourth quarter. But Jay Cutler's fourth-down touchdown pass to Eddie Royal pulled Denver within one point with 24 seconds remaining, and the Broncos went for two points instead of sending the game to overtime. Cutler and Royal teamed again on the winning conversion.

Ronnie Brown burned the Patriots in Week 3.

4 INDIANAPOLIS 31, Houston 27 (Week 5)

The Colts were struggling early in the season and looked as if they would fall to 1–3 while trailing the Texans 27–10 with just a little more than four minutes left in the game. But Indianapolis scored three touchdowns in only 130 seconds to pull off a stunning comeback. The winning points came on Peyton Manning's five-yard touchdown pass to Reggie Wayne with 1:54 to go.

5 MIAMI 38, New England 13 (Week 3)

This was the game that launched the "Wildcat" craze. The Dolphins, who won only one game all of 2007, had started 2008 with back-to-back losses. But they stunned New England when Ronnie Brown ran for four touchdowns and passed for another. All but one of those scores came on direct snaps to the Miami running back.

The Giants and Steelers had a classic defensive battle in Week 8.

6 CAROLINA 33, New Orleans 31 (Week 17)

The Panthers needed a victory to clinch the NFC South title, and they built a 30–10 lead in the fourth quarter. Saints QB Drew Brees rallied his team by passing for three touchdowns in the final period for a 31–30 lead. Finally, John Kasay kicked a 42-yard field goal with one second left to give Carolina the division championship.

7 ARIZONA 30, Dallas 24 (Week 6, overtime)

The Cowboys looked as if they were the team to beat early in the 2008 season, but the Cardinals' thrilling victory signaled a change in the NFC power structure. Dallas rallied to send the game into overtime by scoring 10 points in the final two minutes of the fourth quarter. But a blocked punt that was recovered in the end zone won it for Arizona after only one minute of extra time.

8 N.Y. GIANTS 21, Pittsburgh 14 (Week 8)

This midseason contest was for fans of physical, hard-nosed football. The defending Super Bowl–champion Giants and the eventual Super Bowl–champion Steelers slugged it out for four quarters at Heinz Field in Pittsburgh. The Giants' defense posted four interceptions, five sacks, and a safety before the offense provided the winning points on Eli Manning's two-yard pass to Kevin Boss with 3:11 left.

9 N.Y. JETS 34, New England 31 (Week 11, overtime)

The Patriots marched 80 yards in the last minute of the fourth quarter to send the game into overtime. They tied it when Matt Cassel fired a fourth-down, 16-yard strike to Randy Moss with one second remaining. In overtime, though, Jets quarterback Brett Favre never let New England get the ball. He marched his team 64 yards in 14 plays to the winning field goal.

10 PITTSBURGH 11, San Diego 10 (Week 11)

Okay, it really wasn't a pretty game to watch. But after Jeff Reed kicked the winning field goal from 32 yards with 11 seconds left, it created the first 11–10 final score ever. That's in nearly 13,000 games!

A SUPER SUPER BOWL

The Pittsburgh Steelers played the Arizona Cardinals in Super Bowl XLIII in Tampa, Florida, on February 1, 2009 . . . and for once the game lived up to the immense hype. Wide receiver Santonio Holmes's six-yard touchdown catch with 42 seconds left capped a last-ditch, 78-yard drive that lifted the Steelers to a 27–23 victory.

Holmes's big catch was just one of a series of amazing plays that kept the 70,774 fans at Raymond James Stadium on the edge of their seats and millions of viewers glued to their television sets.

"Harrison is a great player—that's why he's the defensive MVP. Guys like that make big plays on the big stage."

— STEELERS SAFETY TROY POLAMALU

Warner rallied his team late in the game . . .

The first of the big moments came on the final play of the first half. Arizona trailed just 10–7 and looked as if it might take the lead after marching to Pittsburgh's one-yard line 18 seconds before halftime. But when Kurt Warner tried to flip a short pass into the end zone, Steelers linebacker James Harrison stepped in front of the toss and intercepted the ball. Harrison headed to the opposite end zone, 100 yards away, with several Cardinals players in hot pursuit. Larry Fitzgerald finally caught up to him on the right sideline near Arizona's goal line. Fitzgerald tried to tackle Harrison, but both players tumbled into the end zone. Touchdown!

Trailing 17–7, the Cardinals were down, but not out. It was 20–7 in the fourth quarter before Fitzgerald caught

. . . but in the end, Pittsburgh's Roethlisberger hoisted the trophy.

a one-yard touchdown pass with 7:33 left. That made it 20–14. A safety made it 20–16 before Arizona took over possession on its 36-yard line with 2:58 to go. On the second play from there, Warner threw a short pass over the middle to Fitzgerald, who was running free. He split the Steelers' secondary line and raced 64 yards without being touched. Suddenly, the Cardinals led 23–20.

Pittsburgh had one final chance beginning at its 22-yard line with 2:30 remaining in the game. A couple of passes from Ben Roethlisberger to Holmes helped move the ball near midfield. Then, Roethlisberger tossed a short pass to Holmes, who zigged and zagged his way to the Cardinals' six-yard line. Two plays later, Big Ben lofted a pass in between three Arizona defenders into the back corner of the end zone. Holmes latched on and kept his feet inbounds. The Steelers won 27–23 for their record sixth Super Bowl title.

Holmes was named the game's MVP after catching 9 passes for 131 yards. For the Cardinals, Warner passed for 377 yards and 3 touchdowns. Fitzgerald had 7 catches for 127 yards and 2 TDs.

BOX SCORE

Pittsburgh	**3**	**14**	**3**	**7**	**—**	**27**
Arizona	**0**	**7**	**0**	**16**	**—**	**23**

Pit–FG Reed 18

Pit–Russell 1 run (Reed kick)

Ari–Patrick 1 pass from Warner (Rackers kick)

Pit–Harrison 100 interception return (Reed kick)

Pit–FG Reed 21

Ari–Fitzgerald 1 pass from Warner (Rackers kick)

Ari–Safety, Steelers penalized for holding in the end zone

Ari–Fitzgerald 64 pass from Warner (Rackers kick)

Pit–Holmes 6 pass from Roethlisberger (Reed kick)

SIDELINE TO SIDELINE

Madden Retires

You know John Madden from his way-cool video games, and maybe from his work as a football analyst on TV. But did you know that before those jobs, Madden also was one of the most successful head coaches ever? In April, Madden retired after more than 40 years in the NFL.

Um . . . First, a Win Would Be Nice

The Detroit Lions set an NFL record for futility in the 2008 season by losing every game they played. The 1976 Tampa Bay Buccaneers were the only other team to do that in the Super Bowl era, but they played only 14 games. The Lions managed it despite playing 16 games. Still, that didn't stop star running back Kevin Smith from guaranteeing a play-off berth in the 2009 season. We're a little skeptical.

A Record That Never Can Be Broken

Things didn't look good for the Vikings when they were backed up at their own one-yard line in the second quarter of a game against the Bears in Week 13. But quarterback Gus Frerotte heaved a pass as far as he could down the left sideline, and speedy receiver Bernard Berrian caught the ball in stride. He raced to the end zone to complete a record-tying, 99-yard touchdown pass and spark a 34–14 victory.

FAVRE PACKS BAGS; JETS TO VIKINGS!

The never-ending "retirement" of all-time NFL passing leader Brett Favre continues in 2009. First he left Green Bay after the 2007 season, his place in history assured, his name all over the record book. Then he decided to come back and play one more season for the New York Jets. Then he "retired" again. Surprise! He's back, only this time he'll haunt his former team as the leader of their NFC Central rivals, the Minnesota Vikings. Is this the end? Or does Favre have one more retirement in him?

Fantasy Football: Rookies Rule!

It's generally a good idea to stay away from rookies when drafting your fantasy team. They usually take a little time to get up to speed in the NFL. Not in 2008, though. A whole bunch of first-year players made their fantasy owners (and their real-life NFL owners) happy, especially running backs like the Bears' Matt Forté, the Texans' Steve Slaton, the Panthers' Jonathan Stewart, and the Titans' Chris Johnson. If history is any indication, though, don't expect so much from rookies in 2009. A few that might have an impact: Jets quarterback Mark Sanchez, 49ers wide receiver Michael Crabtree, and Broncos running back Knowshon Moreno.

Wildcats Everywhere

Early in the season, the Dolphins unveiled a surprise formation in which the ball was snapped directly to running back Ronnie Brown instead of to quarterback Chad Pennington. It worked so well–sparking a 38–13 rout of the Patriots the first time it was used–that teams all over the league came up with their own version of what Miami called the "Wildcat" offense.

Two Times 1,000

The New York Giants were so good at running the ball in 2008 that they had two 1,000 rushers: Brandon Jacobs (1,089 yards) and Derrick Ward (1,025 yards). That was only the fourth time in league history that teammates each topped 1,000 yards on the ground in the same season.

Three Times 1,000

Three 1,000-yard receivers on the same team is almost as rare as two 1,000-yard rushers. The 2008 Cardinals were only the fifth team ever to do it: Larry Fitzgerald (1,431), Anquan Boldin (1,038), and Steve Breaston (1,006).

Aloha Means Goodbye

Well, maybe not forever. But after 30 years in Honolulu, the Pro Bowl–the NFL's annual all-star game–moved to Miami for the 2009 season. The idea is that the Pro Bowl will draw more attention in the Super Bowl host city the week before the Big Game than in Hawaii the week after it. Still, the NFL didn't rule out the possibility of a return to the islands someday.

Brady Out, Cassel In

Less than a quarter into the 2008 season, New England lost star quarterback Tom Brady for the year with a knee injury. Backup Matt Cassel filled in nicely, passing for 3,693 yards, but New England missed the play-offs one year after making it to the Super Bowl.

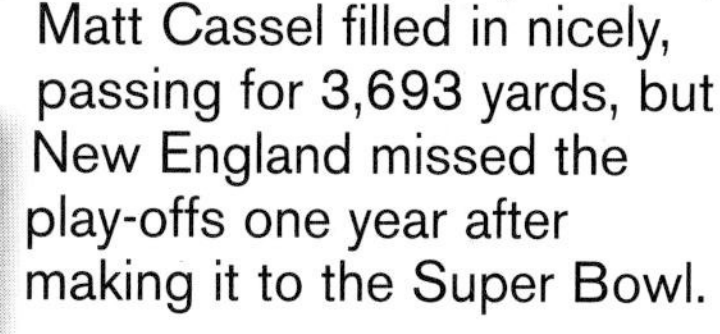

What's in a Name?

Cincinnati Pro Bowl wide receiver Chad Johnson legally changed his name to Chad Ochocinco in 2008, and had his poorest season since his rookie year in 2001. Hmmm . . . Bengals fans might want Chad Johnson back.

CLASS OF 2009

When he was in college at Purdue, Rod Woodson was called "Superman" because he did it all: He played offense, defense, and special teams. After joining Pittsburgh as a first-round draft choice in 1987, Woodson returned kicks for a little while in addition to playing cornerback. But the Steelers knew that he was too valuable, and he stuck to defense the rest of his career. (He eventually switched to safety.) Woodson played for four teams in 17 seasons. He intercepted 71 passes, and he returned a record 12 of them for touchdowns. He made the Pro Bowl 11 times. In 2009, he headlined the Pro Football Hall of Fame's induction class. Here's the Class of 2009:

TWO FOR 2010 Who will be in the Class of 2010, announced the day before Super Bowl XLIV in South Florida? Well, two shoo-ins that are eligible for the first time are Emmitt Smith (the NFL's all-time leading rusher) and Jerry Rice (the all-time leading pass catcher). They can book their trip to Canton for the induction ceremonies next summer.

Bob Hayes, WR
Dallas (1965–1974), San Francisco (1975)

Randall McDaniel, G
Minnesota (1988–1999), Tampa Bay (2000–01)

Bruce Smith, DE
Buffalo (1985–1999), Washington (2000–03)

Derrick Thomas, LB
Kansas City (1989–1999)

Ralph Wilson Jr., Owner
Buffalo (1960–present)

◀◀Rod Woodson, CB/S
Pittsburgh (1987–1996), San Francisco (1997), Baltimore (1998–2001), Oakland (2002–2003)

TOMORROW'S LEGENDS TODAY

Which players who made their NFL debuts in 2008 might be headed to the Hall of Fame in, say, 2025 or so? No one has that good of a crystal ball! But here are several young stars who can dream big:

JAKE LONG, T, MIAMI ▶▶▶

The top pick in the 2008 draft justified the Dolphins' faith in him by making the Pro Bowl in his rookie season.

MATT RYAN, QB, ATLANTA

The Falcons' signal caller earned as much praise for his poise and leadership during his rookie season as he did for his strong throwing arm.

DARREN McFADDEN, RB, OAKLAND

He didn't put up big numbers as a rookie in 2008, but there is nothing that the versatile back can't do on the football field.

MATT FORTÉ, RB, CHICAGO

Forté was a one-man show for the Bears in 2008, when he led the team in both rushing yards and receptions.

DOMINIQUE RODGERS-CROMARTIE, CB, ARIZONA

It's no surprise that the Cardinals' defensive backfield started playing a whole lot better after Rodgers-Cromartie cracked the starting lineup midway through his rookie year.

"This is a spot where you hopefully want to end up. I think it definitely inspires us all."

— JAKE LONG, AFTER TOURING THE HALL OF FAME

NEW FOR 2009

THE ENVELOPE, PLEASE

Actually, there was little suspense in the top choice for the 2009 NFL draft. The Detroit Lions, who used five QBs in their 0–16 season, agreed to contract terms with University of Georgia signal caller Matthew Stafford before the draft even got under way. It was the seventh time in the decade of the 2000s that a quarterback went No. 1.

CHOICE	PLAYER	POSITION	TEAM
1.	Matthew Stafford	QB	Detroit
2.	Jason Smith	T	St. Louis
3.	Tyson Jackson	DE	Kansas City
4.	Aaron Curry	LB	Seattle
5.	Mark Sanchez	QB	N.Y. Jets
6.	Andre Smith	T	Cincinnati
7.	Darrius Heyward-Bey	WR	Oakland
8.	Eugene Monroe	T	Jacksonville
9.	B. J. Raji	DT	Green Bay
10.	Michael Crabtree	WR	San Francisco
11.	Aaron Maybin	DE	Buffalo
12.	Knowshon Moreno	RB	Denver
13.	Brian Orakpo	DE	Washington
14.	Malcolm Jenkins	CB	New Orleans
15.	Brian Cushing	LB	Houston
16.	Larry English	DE	San Diego
17.	Josh Freeman	QB	Tampa Bay
18.	Robert Ayers	LB	Denver
19.	Jeremy Maclin	WR	Philadelphia
20.	Brandon Pettigrew	TE	Detroit
21.	Alex Mack	C	Cleveland
22.	Percy Harvin	WR	Minnesota
23.	Michael Oher	T	Baltimore
24.	Peria Jerry	DT	Atlanta
25.	Vontae Davis	CB	Miami
26.	Clay Matthews	LB	Green Bay
27.	Donald Brown	RB	Indianapolis
28.	Eric Wood	C	Buffalo
29.	Hakeem Nicks	WR	N.Y. Giants
30.	Kenny Britt	WR	Tennessee
31.	Chris Wells	RB	Arizona
32.	Evander Hood	DT	Pittsburgh

Safety First

NFL owners approved several rules changes for 2009. Most of them, however, were intended to increase player safety and won't easily be noticed when watching a game. Look closely at kickoffs, though. The return man can't run behind a blocking wall of more than two players anymore. The days of a three- or four-man "wedge" are over . . . much to the relief of the wedge-buster on the kicking team!

New (and Improved?)

After losing every game in 2008, the Lions figured it was time for a new look. So they unveiled a new logo and new uniforms for 2009. Hey, it can't hurt, right?

The San Francisco 49ers will also don new threads in 2009. Their new uniforms look a lot like their old ones, though–as in their 1980s uniforms. The bright red of that decade was more popular with fans than the darker red of recent seasons. Maybe because it reminds them of the team's dynasty years.

Big D ▲

There's an old saying that goes, "Everything's bigger in Texas." Apparently, that includes NFL stadiums. After playing 38 seasons in Texas Stadium in Irving, Texas, the Dallas Cowboys moved into a new home in Arlington, Texas, in 2009.

The three-million-square-foot Dallas Cowboys Stadium, which has a seating capacity of up to 100,000, is the largest NFL stadium ever built. Even before the new stadium opened its doors, it was awarded a Super Bowl: Game XLV will be played in February 2011.

AND THE WINNER IS . . .

Even before Dallas hosts Super Bowl XLV, we think the team will make it to Super Bowl XLIV in February 2010. The Cowboys were the NFL's best team early in the 2008 season before a disastrous stretch run left them out of the play-offs. They are our pick to win it all in the 2009 season. What team is your choice?

★**Dallas Cowboys**★

Now fill in the team you think will win (no fair writing if Super Bowl XLIV has already happened!). Good luck!

____

FOR THE RECORD

All-Time Super Bowl Winners

GAME	SEASON	WINNING TEAM	LOSING TEAM	SCORE	SITE
I	1966	**Green Bay**	Kansas City	**35–10**	Los Angeles
II	1967	**Green Bay**	Oakland	**33–14**	Miami
III	1968	**N.Y. Jets**	Baltimore	**16–7**	Miami
IV	1969	**Kansas City**	Minnesota	**23–7**	New Orleans
V	1970	**Baltimore**	Dallas	**16–13**	Miami
VI	1971	**Dallas**	Miami	**24–3**	New Orleans
VII	1972	**Miami**	Washington	**14–7**	Los Angeles
VIII	1973	**Miami**	Minnesota	**24–7**	Houston
IX	1974	**Pittsburgh**	Minnesota	**16–6**	New Orleans
X	1975	**Pittsburgh**	Dallas	**21–17**	Miami
XI	1976	**Oakland**	Minnesota	**32–14**	Pasadena
XII	1977	**Dallas**	Denver	**27–10**	New Orleans
XIII	1978	**Pittsburgh**	Dallas	**35–31**	Miami
XIV	1979	**Pittsburgh**	Los Angeles	**31–19**	Pasadena
XV	1980	**Oakland**	Philadelphia	**27–10**	New Orleans
XVI	1981	**San Francisco**	Cincinnati	**26–21**	Pontiac, Mich.
XVII	1982	**Washington**	Miami	**27–17**	Pasadena
XVIII	1983	**L.A. Raiders**	Washington	**38–9**	Tampa
XIX	1984	**San Francisco**	Miami	**38–16**	Stanford

GAME	SEASON	WINNING TEAM	LOSING TEAM	SCORE	SITE
XX	1985	**Chicago**	New England	**46–10**	New Orleans
XXI	1986	**N.Y. Giants**	Denver	**39–20**	Pasadena
XXII	1987	**Washington**	Denver	**42–10**	San Diego
XXIII	1988	**San Francisco**	Cincinnati	**20–16**	South Florida
XXIV	1989	**San Francisco**	Denver	**55–10**	New Orleans
XXV	1990	**N.Y. Giants**	Buffalo	**20–19**	Tampa
XXVI	1991	**Washington**	Buffalo	**37–24**	Minneapolis
XXVII	1992	**Dallas**	Buffalo	**52–17**	Pasadena
XXVIII	1993	**Dallas**	Buffalo	**30–13**	Atlanta
XXIX	1994	**San Francisco**	San Diego	**49–26**	South Florida
XXX	1995	**Dallas**	Pittsburgh	**27–17**	Tempe
XXXI	1996	**Green Bay**	New England	**35–21**	New Orleans
XXXII	1997	**Denver**	Green Bay	**31–24**	San Diego
XXXIII	1998	**Denver**	Atlanta	**34–19**	South Florida
XXXIV	1999	**St. Louis**	Tennessee	**23–16**	Atlanta
XXXV	2000	**Baltimore**	N.Y. Giants	**34–7**	Tampa
XXXVI	2001	**New England**	St. Louis	**20–17**	New Orleans
XXXVII	2002	**Tampa Bay**	Oakland	**48–21**	San Diego
XXXVIII	2003	**New England**	Carolina	**32–29**	Houston
XXXIX	2004	**New England**	Philadelphia	**24–21**	Jacksonville
XL	2005	**Pittsburgh**	Seattle	**21–10**	Detroit
XLI	2006	**Indianapolis**	Chicago	**29–17**	South Florida
XLII	2007	**N.Y. Giants**	New England	**17–14**	Glendale, Ariz.
XLIII	2008	**Pittsburgh**	Arizona	**27–23**	Tampa

COLLEGE FOOTBALL

THE PLAY OF THE YEAR!
Michael Crabtree of Texas Tech stunned the No. 1-ranked Texas Longhorns when he scored here on the last play of their game in October 2008. Tech's high-flying offense had a miracle in its bag to pull off the stunning 39–33 upset, scuttling the Longhorns' title hopes . . . or did it?

The Texas Longhorns hoist the "Golden Hat" trophy after beating rival Oklahoma.

THREE FOR ONE

In September 2008, Florida was shocked on its home turf (known as "The Swamp") by Mississippi. After the loss, Tebow spoke briefly. Fighting back tears, the guy with the biggest heart in his sport promised Gators fans that "you will never see a team play harder than we will the rest of the season."

One loss is usually all it takes to lose your shot at a national title. The Gators seemed cooked by October 1. So did USC, which got rolled by underdog Oregon State and its 5-foot 7-inch freshman tailback, Jacquizz Rodgers, 27–21, in a game in Corvallis.

With Florida and USC out of the picture, attention turned to the Big 12. First, Colt McCoy and Texas outdrew Sam Bradford and No. 1-ranked Oklahoma, 45–35, in the most exciting game of the season to date.

A few weeks later, Graham Harrell and Texas Tech lassoed the No. 1 Longhorns with a touchdown pass on the final play to win, 39–33. And suddenly, that was the season's most thrilling contest.

A few weeks after that, Oklahoma ambushed the Red Raiders, 65–21. Now all three teams had the same record of 11–1. Which of the three schools deserved to play for the national title? Which of the three quarterbacks deserved to win the Heisman Trophy?

Harrell, of Texas Tech, completed the most passes (442) of anyone in the nation and ended his career with more touchdown passes (134) than any player in major college football history. Bradford, of Oklahoma, threw the most TD passes (50) and Texas's McCoy had the highest completion percentage (77%).

Oklahoma, Texas, or Texas Tech? Bradford, McCoy, or Harrell? There was no right answer, because there was no wrong answer. In the end, perhaps because the Sooners left the best final impression, Bradford won the Heisman and Oklahoma earned a spot in the national championship game.

The Gators, meanwhile, held true to their leader's pledge. Florida played harder–and better–than every other team the rest of the way. Florida knocked off No. 1 Alabama in the SEC championship game, then stymied the explosive Sooners, 24–14, in the national championship game.

FINAL 2008 TOP 10

(From the Associated Press)

1. **Florida**
2. **Utah**
3. **USC**
4. **Texas**
5. **Oklahoma**
6. **Alabama**
7. **Texas Christian**
8. **Penn State**
9. **Ohio State**
10. **Oregon**

Battle of the Coaches!

Along with the great games on the field, another duel was taking place–this one was between two of the oldest guys in the game. Bobby Bowden, the 78-year-old coach at Florida State, began the season with 373 wins, the most in NCAA Football Bowl Subdivision (FBS) history. Penn State coach Joe Paterno, 81, had 371. "Joe Pa" had hip surgery in the middle of the season, but he still led the Nittany Lions to a 12–1 record and overtook Bowden in all-time victories, 383 to 382. That's where it stands heading into 2009.

2008 MAJOR BOWL RESULTS

Tostitos Fiesta Bowl

Texas 24, Ohio State 21

Allstate Sugar Bowl

Utah 31, Alabama 17

◀Rose Bowl

USC 38, Penn State 24

Cotton Bowl

Mississippi 47, Texas Tech 34

FedEx Orange Bowl

Virginia Tech 20, Cincinnati 7

Small Schools=Big Winners

The teams in the Football Bowl Subdivision get all the attention, but these schools reached the top of lower-level football divisions in 2008.

Football Championship Subdivision

Richmond 24, Montana 7 ▶▶▶

Division II

Minnesota Duluth 21, Northwest Missouri State 14

Division III

Mount Union 31, Wisconsin-Whitewater 26

Here They Go Again!

"Déjà vu" is a French term that means "already seen." The 2008 season's BCS Championship Game (played in Miami's Dolphin Stadium in January 2009) certainly had that sense to it.

The Florida Gators were attempting to win their second national title of the past three seasons. The Oklahoma Sooners were attempting to avoid losing a national title game in this very stadium for the second time in five seasons. The Sooners had played in the BCS Championship Game in 2005, and then, as in this game, the contest pitted a pair of quarterbacks who had each already won the Heisman Trophy.

Sam Bradford, the reigning Heisman winner, led an Oklahoma offense that had scored at least 60 points in each of its previous five games. Tim Tebow, the 2007 Heisman honoree, led a Gator offense that had just knocked off top-ranked Alabama in the SEC Championship Game.

The game hinged on a pair of interceptions by the Gators. Just before halftime, with the score tied 7–7, Bradford's short pass was intercepted at the goal line by Florida's Major Wright. In the fourth quarter, Bradford seemed to hit wideout Juaquin Iglesias on a post pattern, but Gator safety Ahmad Black wrestled the ball away.

"That was the turning point," said Gator coach Urban Meyer after Florida won 24–14. The Gators were national champions!

Tim Tebow ran and passed the Gators to another title.

CHALK TALK

Here's our take on the top moments from the 2008 college football season.

1. Longhorns Come Up Short Texas Tech ends Texas's dream of an undefeated season, and quarterback Colt McCoy's shot at the Heisman Trophy, with a 39–33 victory. The game-winning touchdown pass came with :01 remaining. It was the game, and the play, of the season.

◄◄◄2. Utah Goes 13–0 At 12–0, Utah is the only school to finish the regular season undefeated. But the Utes, who do not play in a major conference, entered the Sugar Bowl against 12–1 Alabama as heavy underdogs. They outplayed the Crimson Tide from the opening snap and won by two touchdowns. The 31–17 final score wasn't even that close.

3. Tim Tebow's Pledge After Florida suffers a shocking home loss to Mississippi early in the season, quarterback Tim Tebow tells fans, "I'm sorry. Extremely sorry. But I promise you one thing: A lot of good will come from this. You will never see a player, in the entire country, play as hard as I will play the rest of the season. You will never see someone push the rest of the team as hard as I will push everybody the rest of the season. And you will never see a team play harder than we will play the rest of the season. God bless." Now here's a guy who keeps his promises. The Gators did not lose again and wound up beating Oklahoma for the national title.

4. Joe Paterno Passes Bobby Bowden In his 82nd year—and 43rd season as head coach at Penn State—Joe Paterno passes Bobby Bowden, the head coach at Florida State, on the all-time wins list for FBS head coaches.

5. Washington Weak in Review The poor Huskies. U-Dub was the only team not to win a game. The Huskies also lost their best player, quarterback Jake Locker, to a broken thumb when he was attempting to make a block. Earlier in the season, Locker was the victim of the season's most controversial penalty when he was flagged for excessively celebrating a potential game-tying TD as time expired. All Jake did was toss the ball in the air. They say every dog has his day, but these Huskies never did.

6. Death Valley Daze (or, Troy Story) Tiny Troy University visited LSU, whose notoriously noisy stadium has been dubbed "Death Valley," for what was certain to be a massacre. And for nearly three quarters, it was. Troy led the defending national champions 31-3! Then the Tigers woke up and scored 37 points in 17 minutes to avoid the upset and win 40–31.

7. Ugly Injury The sideline is supposed to be safe. However, that is where the ugliest hit of the season took place. Notre Dame's John Ryan, running downfield after a punt, was blocked into his head coach, Charlie Weis. The Fighting Irish coach was watching the ball and never saw Ryan ram into him. Charlie's left knee bent in a direction knees aren't supposed to bend, not even in South Bend. He coached on crutches for weeks after.

8. Rhodes to Success Florida State safety Myron Rolle is a terrific football player and an even better student. Last November, Rolle interviewed to become a Rhodes Scholar, which is as prestigious as it gets, in Alabama. That same night, he took the field for the Seminoles when they played at Maryland. Florida State lost the football game, but Myron was awarded the two-year scholarship.

9. Green Daze Kryptonite is green, as is much of the state of heavily forested Oregon. What kryptonite is to Superman, Oregon is to Southern California. The top-ranked Trojans lost at unranked Oregon State in September, making them 0–3 in the Beaver State the last three years. Outside Oregon, USC was 34–2 in that same period of time.

10. Operation Dumb Drop There was only one problem with North Carolina's plan to have a skydiver land at midfield with the game ball before the Tar Heels' season-opener against The Citadel: He landed inside the football stadium at Duke, Carolina's arch-rival, which is located eight miles away.

FIVE MEMORABLE PLAYS

Crabtree's Catch

1 Imagine scoring the winning touchdown against the top-ranked team in the nation with just one second to play. Texas Tech wideout Michael Crabtree doesn't have to: He did it on a 28-yard catch against No. 1 Texas in the season's most dramatic game and finish.

Zebras Tackle, Too

3 Wilbur Hackett was a fine linebacker at Kentucky in 1970. These days he is a referee, which is why it was so bizarre when he accidentally tackled South Carolina quarterback Stephen Garcia on the five-yard line in a game against LSU.

OW!-L Play

4 In his first two seasons as the Texas quarterback, Colt McCoy had a reputation for being fragile. That all ended in a single play against Rice. Colt scrambled out of the pocket and arrived at the goal line at the same time as Owl defensive back Andrew Sendejo. McCoy bulldozed Sendejo, who fell to his knees, and then Colt hit him again. Can a quarterback be flagged for a flagrant hit while carrying the ball?

Now That's Scary

5 What would you do if a football player, running full speed, flew right into the front row and into your lap? That's what happened to seven-year-old Garrett Monroe when Cincinnati receiver Mardy Gilyard tried to catch a pass and fell into him. Garrett was upset, but Gilyard picked up the young fan and gave him a big hug until he was satisfied that Garrett was okay. Gilyard later scored a TD in the Bearcats' 24–10 upset of South Florida.

Knowshon's Leap ▲

2 Georgia tailback Knowshon Moreno may not be able to leap tall buildings in a single bound, but he made a habit of leaping straight over defensive backs. On his way to a touchdown in a game against Central Michigan, Knowshon hurdled a defender as if he were the backyard fence. As this picture shows, he jumped so fast, even the camera couldn't catch all of him!

BY THE NUMBERS

FBS leaders in various statistical categories:

50 TOUCHDOWN PASSES

Sam BRADFORD, Oklahoma

5,111 PASSING YARDS

Graham HARRELL, Texas Tech

2,083 RUSHING YARDS

Donald BROWN, Connecticut

1,538 RECEIVING YARDS

Austin COLLIE, Brigham Young

113 RECEPTIONS

Casey FITZGERALD, North Texas State

22 TOUCHDOWNS

Javon RINGER, Michigan State

MiQuale LEWIS, Ball State

133 POINTS

Jeff Wolfert, Missouri

24 FIELD GOALS

Graham Gano, Florida State; **Ryan Harrison,** Air Force Academy

"BIG SIX" CHAMPS

◄◄◄Atlantic Coast Conference (ACC)

Virginia Tech (10-4 overall, 5–3 conference)
The Hokies avenged a midseason defeat at Boston College to rout the Eagles 30–12 in the conference title game. Then they capped their season with a 20–7 upset of No. 12 Cincinnati in the Orange Bowl.

Big East **Cincinnati (11–3, 6–1)**

In just their fourth season in the Big East, the Bearcats won their first championship. They blasted Syracuse 30–10 in their conference finale to win their championship and reach 10 total victories for the second year in a row.

Big Ten **Penn State (11–2, 7–1)**

Only a last-second, one-point loss at Iowa in the 10th game kept the Nittany Lions from playing for the national championship. Legendary coach Joe Paterno's squad featured a high-powered offense that averaged 38.2 points per game.

Big 12 **Oklahoma (12–2, 7–1)**

The Sooners outlasted high-powered Texas and Texas Tech to win the South Division of the nation's most exciting conference. Then Oklahoma, which scored 50 or more points 10 times, pasted North champion Missouri 62–21 in the conference title game.

Pacific-10 Conference (Pac-10) **USC (12–1, 8–1)**

A 52–7 win at Virginia in the season opener vaulted the Trojans to the top of the polls, but an upset loss at Oregon State in Game 3 kept them from the national-title game. Still, a 38–24 victory over Penn State in the Rose Bowl gave USC its record seventh consecutive Top 4 finish (No. 3) in the Associated Press poll.

Southeastern Conference (SEC) **Florida (7–1, 13–1)**

The Gators overcame a one-point home loss to Mississippi early in the season (see "Tim Tebow's Pledge" on page 62) to win their last 10 games, including a 24–14 victory over Oklahoma for the BCS national championship.

Heisman Sooner or Later

Sam Bradford became the second straight sophomore–and only second ever–to win the Heisman Trophy. The Oklahoma quarterback wanted to add a national title to his hardware haul, but his team lost to 2007 Heisman winner Tim Tebow and Florida. Bradford had an amazing season, though, with 48 touchdown passes and only six interceptions. His 84 TD passes in 2007–08 are the most ever for a player in his first two college seasons, too.

Bradford was the fifth Sooner to win the award, the most recent being quarterback Jason White in 2003. As Tebow did in 2008, Bradford will return in 2009 with a chance to become only the second player ever with a pair of Heisman Trophies. Trivia time: Who is the only player with matching Heismans? (Answer below.)

Trivia answer: Archie Griffin of Ohio State won in both 1974 and 1975.

What's Up in 2009?

For the 2009 college football season, a lot of players will return, including, for the first time ever, the two most recent Heisman Trophy winners: Sam Bradford of Oklahoma and Tim Tebow of Florida.

Tebow's Gators and Bradford's Sooners will both be favored to return to the BCS Championship Game, which will be held at the Rose Bowl in Pasadena in January 2010. Look out, though, for quarterback Colt McCoy and Texas. The Longhorns felt they belonged in the title game last season, and no squad will be more motivated.

On the rise? Oklahoma State, Mississippi, and resurgent Notre Dame. Also, don't be surprised if the best running back in the country is a man named Best: California tailback Jahvid Best (left).

WE'RE NO.1

These are the teams to finish atop the Associated Press's final rankings since the poll first was introduced in 1936.

SEASON	TEAM	RECORD
1936	**Minnesota**	7–1
1937	**Pittsburgh**	9–0–1
1938	**Texas Christian**	11–0
1939	**Texas A & M**	11–0
1940	**Minnesota**	8–0
1941	**Minnesota**	8–0
1942	**Ohio State**	9–1
1943	**Notre Dame**	9–1
1944	**Army**	9–0
1945	**Army**	9–0
1946	**Notre Dame**	8–0–1
1947	**Notre Dame**	9–0
1948	**Michigan**	9–0
1949	**Notre Dame**	10–0
1950	**Oklahoma**	10–1
1951	**Tennessee**	10–1
1952	**Michigan State**	9–0
1953	**Maryland**	10–1
1954	**Ohio State**	10–0
1955	**Oklahoma**	11–0
1956	**Oklahoma**	10–0
1957	**Auburn**	10–0
1958	**LSU**	11–0
1959	**Syracuse**	11–0
1960	**Minnesota**	8–2
1961	**Alabama**	11–0
1962	**USC**	11–0
1963	**Texas**	11–0
1964	**Alabama**	10–1
1965	**Alabama**	9–1–1
1966	**Notre Dame**	9–0–1
1967	**USC**	10–1
1968	**Ohio State**	10–0
1969	**Texas**	11–0
1970	**Nebraska**	11–0–1
1971	**Nebraska**	13–0
1972	**USC**	12–0
1973	**Notre Dame**	11–0
1974	**Oklahoma**	11–0
1975	**Oklahoma**	11–1
1976	**Pittsburgh**	12–0
1977	**Notre Dame**	11–1
1978	**Alabama**	11–1
1979	**Alabama**	12–0
1980	**Georgia**	12–0
1981	**Clemson**	12–0
1982	**Penn State**	11–1
1983	**Miami**	11–1
1984	**Brigham Young**	13–0
1985	**Oklahoma**	11–1
1986	**Penn State**	12–0
1987	**Miami**	12–0
1988	**Notre Dame**	12–0
1989	**Miami**	11–1
1990	**Colorado**	11–1–1
1991	**Miami**	12–0
1992	**Alabama**	13–0
1993	**Florida State**	12–1
1994	**Nebraska**	13–0
1995	**Nebraska**	12–0
1996	**Florida**	12–1
1997	**Michigan**	12–0
1998	**Tennessee**	13–0
1999	**Florida State**	12–0
2000	**Oklahoma**	13–0
2001	**Miami**	12–0
2002	**Ohio State**	14–0
2003	**USC**	12–1
2004	**USC**	13–0
2005	**Texas**	13–0
2006	**Florida**	13–1
2007	**LSU**	10–2
2008	**Florida**	13–1

BCS National Championship Games

College football (at its highest level) is one of the few sports that doesn't have an on-field play-off to determine its champion. In the 1998 season, the sport introduced the Bowl Championship Series (BCS), which tries to pit the two top teams in the title game according to a complicated formula that takes into account records, polls, and computer rankings. Here are the results of the all-time BCS Championship Games:

The Florida Gators celebrate their 2008 win.

SEASON	SCORE	SITE
1998	**Tennessee 23, Florida State 16**	TEMPE, AZ
1999	**Florida State 46, Virginia Tech 29**	NEW ORLEANS, LA
2000	**Oklahoma 13, Florida State 2**	MIAMI, FL
2001	**Miami 37, Nebraska 14**	PASADENA, CA
2002	**Ohio State 31, Miami 24**	TEMPE, AZ
2003	**LSU 21, Oklahoma 14**	NEW ORLEANS, LA
2004	**USC 55, Oklahoma 19**	MIAMI, FL
2005	**Texas 41, USC 38**	PASADENA, CA
2006	**Florida 41, Ohio State 14**	GLENDALE, AZ
2007	**LSU 38, Ohio State 24**	NEW ORLEANS, LA
2008	**Florida 24, Oklahoma 14**	MIAMI, FL

HANSBROUGH
50

COLLEGE BASKETBALL

TO THE HOOP!
North Carolina star Tyler Hansbrough, in action here against Oklahoma, turned down a shot at the NBA to come back for one more college season. It paid off for him when he led his Tar Heels to the NCAA championship.

North Carolina hoists the NCAA championship trophy after beating Michigan State.

THE TAR HEELS ARE BACK!

The 2008–09 college basketball season ended the same way it began: with North Carolina at No. 1. But in between start and finish, the season acted more like a dribbling basketball, as top teams bounced up and down the polls.

The Tar Heels were the preseason No. 1 pick, but the season was far bumpier than they thought it would be. Injuries were a big reason. Tyler Hansbrough, the national Player of the Year in 2007–08, was joined by three other key returning players. Then Hansbrough came down with a shin injury before the season opener and missed four games. As the season went on, Carolina's injury woes just kept coming.

Meanwhile, Oklahoma forward Blake Griffin got early notice as the nation's top player (see page 75). Griffin began the year with six consecutive double-doubles (at least 10 points and rebounds in each game). He finished the season averaging 22.7 points and 14.4 rebounds per game.

The Big East made a case for top conference. Of its 16 teams, 6 finished the year in the Top 25. North Carolina shook off its injury problems to roll to 13 straight wins to start the year, including a 35-point pasting of Michigan State in Detroit in what would turn out to be a preview of the national title game. But that's when the ball started bouncing.

In January, North Carolina lost its No. 1 ranking with a loss to Boston College. Pittsburgh took over in the top spot but was out two weeks later after a loss to Louisville. Wake Forest was No. 1 for two days before being upset by Virginia Tech.

Next came Duke–and bang!–they lost to Wake Forest. Connecticut moved to the top but was gone three weeks later. It seemed as if no team wanted to stay on top for very long! Pitt, UConn, and then finally North Carolina again all took their turns at No. 1 as the regular season wound down. Louisville, in fact, owned the spot when the NCAA tournament brackets were announced.

After an NCAA tournament and Final Four that saw fewer upsets than usual (see page 74 for a full report), North Carolina brought it all back to the beginning when it captured its fifth NCAA national championship. After all the ups and downs of the long season, no one was going to take that No. 1 spot away from them this time.

MEN'S COLLEGE BASKETBALL Final Top 10

1. North Carolina
2. Michigan State
3. Connecticut
4. Villanova
5. Louisville
6. Pittsburgh
7. Oklahoma
8. Missouri
9. Memphis
10. Kansas

Syracuse star guard Jonny Flynn

BEST GAME . . . EVER?

The game took six overtimes and almost four hours, and when it was over it was being called maybe the **greatest game of all time**. On March 28, Syracuse and Connecticut, two top-20 teams and longtime rivals, battled in the longest college basketball game in the shot-clock era. The Huskies overcame a late seven-point deficit to force the first OT and then never trailed in any of the first five OTs. But Syracuse finally pulled away in the sixth overtime to win 127–117 and advance to the semifinals of the Big East Tournament.

NCAA TOURNAMENT REPORT

The strength of the Big East was rewarded when it got three No. 1 seeds in the NCAA tournament (Pitt, Louisville, and UConn), joining the fourth No. 1, North Carolina. Although there were some close calls, the first weekend of the NCAAs was almost entirely upset-free. The top three seeds in each region advanced.

Two Big East teams would make it to the Final Four in Detroit, but Pitt and Louisville lost in the regional finals. Pitt's defeat came at the hands of fellow Big East member Villanova. A stunning coast-to-coast sprint to the basket by Scottie Reynolds with 0.5 seconds left beat the Panthers. The Cardinals were eliminated by Michigan State in the Midwest final.

"The last two minutes were exactly like practice. Creating those habits in practice helped us prepare for that important end-of-the-game situation." — SCOTTIE REYNOLDS

Just in time: Reynolds completes his coast-to-coast game-winner.

North Carolina made it back to the Final Four for the second straight season when they knocked off player of the year Blake Griffin and Oklahoma in the South Regional championship game.

The championship game pitted Michigan State against North Carolina in front of 70,000 fans at Ford Field in Detroit. Many of the fans were wearing white and green for the home-state Spartans. However, North Carolina jumped out to a 10-point lead barely four minutes into the game, and soon led by 20 at 31–11. The Tar Heels were up 21 points at the half, thanks largely to Final Four Most Outstanding Player Wayne

WOODEN AWARD WINNER

Named for legendary coach John Wooden, this honor is considered the highest player award in college hoops. The 2009 winner was Blake Griffin of Oklahoma.

Just as North Carolina was expected to be the best team in the country, Blake Griffin was picked as the nation's best player. Both predictions came true. Griffin's combination of size (6'9", 250 pounds), strength, and quickness made him a man among boys in the college game. His best game came against Texas Tech on Valentine's Day, when he scored 40 points and grabbed 23 rebounds.

Griffin helped the Sooners (which included his older brother Taylor) reach the Elite 8, the first time since 2003 the Sooners had made it that far in the Big Dance. Their loss there, though, was Griffin's last college game. He was taken by the Los Angeles Clippers with the first pick of the 2009 Draft (see page 90).

Ellington, who had 17 points, and Ty Lawson, who had with a title-game-record eight steals. The Tar Heels slowed down in the second half, but their lead never dipped below 13 points, and they won in an 89–72 romp.

The win gave Carolina its fifth national title, and second in five seasons, and fulfilled the lofty hype that had followed the team for the past year. The Tar Heels were rewarded with a trip to the White House, where they met with a former pickup-game partner, President Barack Obama. The president had played with the team during a campaign trip to North Carolina in April 2008, and he then made national headlines before the '09 tourney when he picked the Heels to win the title. Just like everyone else who had long since chosen the Tar Heels as the likely champs, the president turned out to be absolutely correct.

UP NEXT The 2010 NCAA Men's Division I Final Four is scheduled for April 3 and 5 at Lucas Oil Stadium in Indianapolis, Indiana. Indianapolis has been home to other Finals Fours, but this will be the first played at Lucas Oil Stadium, the home of the NFL's Colts, which opened in the fall of 2008. In fact, all of the upcoming Final Fours will be in NFL stadiums: Reliant Stadium in Houston, the Superdome in New Orleans, the Georgia Dome in Atlanta, and Cowboys Stadium in Texas.

IN THE PAINT

Did He Call the Bank?

On November 21, 2008, Xavier's Dante Jackson banked in a shot from half-court to give Xavier a 63–62 win over Virginia Tech. It was the only field goal Jackson had all night, and it came after the Hokies' Jeff Allen had put his team ahead with a layup with 1.9 seconds remaining.

411 x 2

Long distance information—get it? In a December game at Syracuse, Cleveland State's Cedric Jackson made a 60-foot shot at the buzzer to give the Vikings a 72–69 upset of the 11th-ranked Orangemen. Then in March, Alabama's Anthony Brock (that's his heave pictured above) made a half-court shot at the buzzer to beat Tennessee in Knoxville. What made that amazing shot even more remarkable was that Brock wasn't even supposed to be at the game! He had been at his grandmother's funeral the day before, but he made it to the game in time and made the winning shot.

From II to I

North Dakota State was a Division II school in 2008, but in 2009 moved to Division I. An NCAA playoff berth seemed like an impossibility for the school, but Ben Woodside made a jumper with three seconds remaining to give the Bison the Sun Belt championship and a spot in the Big Dance.

First Brother-in-Law

Oregon State, coached by Craig Robinson, who is President Obama's brother-in-law, won the College Basketball Invitational by beating UTEP two games to one in the three-game final series.

Not a Mildcat

Kentucky Wildcat Jodie Meeks was a rare bright spot in a dismal season for Kentucky. Meeks scored 54 points in a big win over Tennessee. The Wildcats guard was named second-team All-America.

One Miss and You're Out

The Kentucky Wildcats missed their first NCAA tournament since 1991, so they fired their coach. Ouch! Billy Gillespie was out, and veteran leader John Calipari was in. Let's hope he gets more time than Gillespie's two seasons.

Did the Scoreboard Fall Asleep?

Penn State 38, Illinois 33

Penn State and Illinois combined to score the fewest points in a Division I game in four years. Penn State shot a measly 28 percent while the Illini shot a sorry 30 percent. Oddly, both teams were actually good: Penn State won the NIT, while Illinois was in the top 25.

Bobby Knight Is Probably Happy

Just seven years after playing in the national title game, normally excellent Indiana suffered the worst season in school history. The Hoosiers went 6–25 under first-year coach Tom Crean.

Michael Who?

The University of North Carolina has produced dozens of top basketball players–including a guy named Michael Jordan–over the past four decades. In 2009, Tyler Hansbrough passed all of them, becoming the school's all-time leading scorer with a final total of 2,872 points.

WOMEN'S HOOPS

Perfection. It's a hard goal, and one that has been achieved by only a handful of teams. In women's college basketball, it's been done three times–and all by one school. Led in 2008–09 by superstar sophomore Maya Moore, the national Player of the Year, the Connecticut Huskies were perfect, finishing at 39–0.

The school won all six of its tournament games by at least 19 points, and defeated fellow Big East squad Louisville 76–54 in the NCAA championship game. It was the Huskies' sixth national title, and their first since 2004.

Maya helped UConn win one "Moore" title.

UConn was never seriously challenged, winning each game by at least 10 points.

Another famous women's hoops program, Tennessee, also grabbed its share of headlines, but for different reasons. The Lady Volunteers had won the last two NCAA championships behind star forward Candace Parker, but with Parker gone to the WNBA, Tennessee struggled.

"We're always looking to the future. [But] now we have time to enjoy this win and all the others."

— UCONN GUARD RENEE MONTGOMERY, AFTER HER TEAM'S VICTORY IN THE NCAA TITLE GAME

Tennessee lost in the first round of the NCAA tournament, the first time it had failed to reach the Sweet 16 in the 28-year history of the women's tournament. The season wasn't a complete loss, however. Coach Pat Summitt became the first Division I coach, male or female, to win 1,000 games when the Lady Vols beat Georgia on February 5 in Knoxville.

Aside from Moore, the best player in the country was Oklahoma's Courtney Paris. A bruising power forward and double-double machine, Paris left school as a four-time All-America and the leading rebounder in the history of women's college basketball. She made her biggest news, though, when she vowed before the NCAA tournament that she would return her scholarship, valued at more than $64,000, if the Sooners did not win the national championship. Oklahoma was defeated in the Final Four, and Paris said she planned to honor her commitment.

Women's NCAA Final Top 10

1. UConn
2. Louisville
3. Stanford
4. Oklahoma
5. Maryland
6. Baylor
7. Texas A&M
8. Vanderbilt
9. Ohio State
10. California

SWISHES!

UConn was not the only women's college team to go undefeated in 2008–09. George Fox, in Newberg, Oregon, capped a 32–0 season by beating Washington University in St. Louis 60–53 in the Division III championship game in Holland, Michigan. George Fox was just the sixth Division III team to post a perfect season, and was the first West Coast school to win the national title in the 28 years of the championship. In women's NCAA Division II, Minnesota State, Mankato won its first national title by beating Franklin Pierce 103–94 in the championship game.

Connecticut's NCAA champs celebrated their national title at the White House in late April. That's a pretty big deal, although it's become a regular stop for championship teams. What really made it special was a private shootaround the UConn players had with President Barack Obama. After the team gave the Commander-in-Chief an autographed No. 1 jersey, President Obama took the squad over to the White House's outdoor court. UConn's players reported that the President showed off a pretty good jump shot!

First Fan Obama got his own UConn jersey.

ALL-TIME CHAMPS

NCAA MEN'S DIVISION I

Florida made it two in a row when they won the title in 2007.

Year	Champion
2009	North Carolina
2008	Kansas
2007	Florida
2006	Florida
2005	North Carolina
2004	Connecticut
2003	Syracuse
2002	Maryland
2001	Duke
2000	Michigan State
1999	Connecticut
1998	Kentucky
1997	Arizona
1996	Kentucky
1995	UCLA
1994	Arkansas
1993	North Carolina
1992	Duke
1991	Duke
1990	UNLV
1989	Michigan
1988	Kansas
1987	Indiana
1986	Louisville
1985	Villanova
1984	Georgetown
1983	NC State
1982	North Carolina
1981	Indiana
1980	Louisville
1979	Michigan State
1978	Kentucky
1977	Marquette
1976	Indiana
1975	UCLA
1974	NC State
1973	UCLA

1972 **UCLA**
1971 **UCLA**
1970 **UCLA**
1969 **UCLA**
1968 **UCLA**
1967 **UCLA**
1966 **Texas Western**
1965 **UCLA**
1964 **UCLA**
1963 **Loyola (Illinois)**
1962 **Cincinnati**
1961 **Cincinnati**
1960 **Ohio State**
1959 **California**
1958 **Kentucky**
1957 **North Carolina**
1956 **San Francisco**
1955 **San Francisco**
1954 **La Salle**
1953 **Indiana**
1952 **Kansas**
1951 **Kentucky**
1950 **City Coll. of N.Y.**
1949 **Kentucky**
1948 **Kentucky**
1947 **Holy Cross**
1946 **Oklahoma A&M**
1945 **Oklahoma A&M**
1944 **Utah**
1943 **Wyoming**
1942 **Stanford**
1941 **Wisconsin**
1940 **Indiana**
1939 **Oregon**

NCAA WOMEN

2009 **Connecticut**
2008 **Tennessee**
2007 **Tennessee**
2006 **Maryland**
2005 **Baylor**
2004 **Connecticut**
2003 **Connecticut**
2002 **Connecticut**
2001 **Notre Dame**
2000 **Connecticut**
1999 **Purdue**
1998 **Tennessee**
1997 **Tennessee**
1996 **Tennessee**
1995 **Connecticut**
1994 **North Carolina**
1993 **Texas Tech**
1992 **Stanford**
1991 **Tennessee**
1990 **Stanford**
1989 **Tennessee**
1988 **Louisiana Tech**
1987 **Tennessee**
1986 **Texas**
1985 **Old Dominion**
1984 **USC**
1983 **USC**
1982 **Louisiana Tech**

orlando magic
LAKERS
7
LAKERS
16
MAGIC
14
24
The

NOTHING BUT NET!
Lakers guard Derek Fisher launches a three-point shot over Orlando's Jameer Nelson in the final seconds of the fourth quarter of Game 4 of the NBA finals in June 2009. Fisher's heave found the bottom of the net, tying the game and forcing overtime. The Lakers later won the game in that OT. Three nights later, they clinched their 15th league title.

THE LAKE, LAKE SHOW

Spurred by a desire to prove that he could win an NBA championship without former teammate Shaquille O'Neal, Los Angeles Lakers guard Kobe Bryant willed his team to an exciting six-game victory over the Orlando Magic in the NBA finals in June 2009.

The league championship was the Lakers' 15th, which trails only the Boston Celtics' 17 crowns in NBA history. It also marked the Lakers' first title since the 2001–02 season. That was the last of three Lakers titles in a row with Bryant and O'Neal, the 7'1", 325-pound center, leading the way. The two players did not get along after that, and O'Neal eventually was traded.

> **"To actually do it and see it all happen, it feels like I'm dreaming right now. I can't believe this moment is here."**
>
> — KOBE BRYANT

For most of the season, it appeared that Bryant and Cleveland's LeBron "King" James–the league's two biggest stars–appeared fated for a clash in the NBA finals in June.

James and the Cavaliers won a league-best 66 games during the regular season. Bryant and the Lakers were just a shade behind with 65 victories. Both teams were almost unbeatable on their own floors (Cleveland went 39–2 at Quicken Loans Arena, and Los Angeles was 36–5 at the Staples Center), so it didn't look as if any challengers would be able to overcome the home court advantage of the No. 1 seeds.

But a funny thing happened to the Cavaliers on their way to the finals. They were thoroughly outplayed by center Dwight Howard and the Orlando Magic. The King was dethroned by the Magic's magic in the Eastern Conference finals.

In his fifth NBA season, Howard–who, like Bryant, joined the NBA straight out of high school–became a household name. At the All-Star Game in February, Howard

Dwight "Superman" Howard emerged in '09.

Kobe Bryant was the NBA finals MVP.

emerged from a phone booth, wearing a Superman cape. Superman averaged 20.6 points per game during the regular season and was the league's top rebounder at 13.8 boards per contest.

Miami guard Dwyane Wade led the league in scoring in 2008–09, when he averaged 30.2 points per game. Wade had little help from his teammates, however, and the Heat could not advance past the opening round of the play-offs.

What happened to the Boston Celtics? They got off to an amazing start by winning 27 of their first 29 games. However, a knee injury to star forward Kevin Garnett eventually ended their hopes for back-to-back championships. The defending NBA champ made it back to the play-offs but won only one series there.

In the end, Bryant's dream of calling a championship his own came true.

2008–09 FINAL STANDINGS

EASTERN CONFERENCE

ATLANTIC DIVISION	W	L
Boston	62	20
Philadelphia	41	41
New Jersey	34	48
Toronto	33	49
New York	32	50

CENTRAL DIVISION	W	L
Cleveland	66	16
Chicago	41	41
Detroit	39	43
Indiana	36	46
Milwaukee	34	48

SOUTHEAST DIVISION	W	L
Orlando	59	23
Atlanta	47	35
Miami	43	39
Charlotte	35	47
Washington	19	63

WESTERN CONFERENCE

SOUTHWEST DIVISION	W	L
San Antonio	54	28
Houston	53	29
Dallas	50	32
New Orleans	49	33
Memphis	24	58

NORTHWEST DIVISION	W	L
Denver	54	28
Portland	54	28
Utah	48	34
Minnesota	24	58
Oklahoma City	23	59

PACIFIC DIVISION	W	L
L.A. Lakers	65	17
Phoenix	46	36
Golden State	29	53
L.A. Clippers	19	63
Sacramento	17	65

THE PLAY-OFFS

After roaring through the 2008–09 regular season with a 65–17 record, the Lakers' championship was not a big surprise. The road to that title, however, was not as smooth as expected. NBA finals MVP Kobe Bryant led the way, but the play of forward Pau Gasol and guard Derek Fisher proved that basketball is not a one-man game.

After an opening-round victory over the Utah Jazz, the Lakers' title hopes were nearly derailed by the Houston Rockets in the next round. Houston engineered upset victories in Games 4 and 6 to force a decisive seventh game. Gasol had a big Game 7, scoring 21 points and pulling down 18 rebounds in an 89–70 victory.

In the Western Conference finals against the Nuggets, the Lakers won in six games, with Bryant scoring 35 points and handing off 10 assists in a 119–92 rout in the finale.

In the East, Orlando rallied from two-games-to-one down to win three consecutive games and take a six-game series from the 76ers. But all eyes were on Cleveland and forward LeBron James, who was looking for his first trip to the finals.

After Cleveland beat Detroit and Atlanta in the opening two rounds without losing a game, the Cavaliers were stunned by a 107–106 loss to Orlando in Game 1 of the Eastern Conference finals. James rescued his team with a memorable, buzzer-beating three-pointer to win Game 2, but the team's relief was short-lived. The Magic won three of the next four games to close out the series.

The most dramatic series of the play-offs came in the opening round. The defending-champion Boston Celtics, hobbled without injured forward Kevin Garnett, were taken to the limit by the upstart Chicago Bulls. Not only did the series go the full seven games, but four of the games went into overtime–one was double overtime and another was triple overtime–and five were decided by three points or fewer. In the end, Boston survived by winning Game 7, 109–99.

The Celtics went seven games again in the next round. This time, though, Hedo Turkoglu scored 25 points and Dwight Howard had 16 rebounds and 5 blocks as

Celebrate in L.A.! The Lakers go nuts at the final buzzer.

PLAY-OFF RESULTS

(Games won in parentheses)

FIRST ROUND

EASTERN CONFERENCE

Orlando OVER **Philadelphia (4-2)**
Cleveland OVER **Detroit (4-0)**
Boston OVER **Chicago (4-3)**
Atlanta OVER **Miami (4-3)**

WESTERN CONFERENCE

L.A. Lakers OVER **Utah (4-1)**
Denver OVER **New Orleans (4-1)**
Houston OVER **Portland (4-2)**
Dallas OVER **San Antonio (4-1)**

CONFERENCE SEMIFINALS

EASTERN CONFERENCE

Orlando OVER **Boston (4-3)**
Cleveland OVER **Atlanta (4-0)**

WESTERN CONFERENCE

L.A. Lakers OVER **Houston (4-3)**
Denver OVER **Dallas (4-1)**

CONFERENCE FINALS

EASTERN CONFERENCE

Orlando OVER **Cleveland (4-2)**

WESTERN CONFERENCE

L.A. Lakers OVER **Denver (4-2)**

NBA FINALS

L.A. Lakers OVER **Orlando (4-1)**

Together Again (Sort Of)

Guard Kobe Bryant (right) and center Shaquille O'Neal teamed to help the Lakers win three NBA titles in a row in the early 2000s before they feuded and O'Neal was traded to Miami in 2004. In February 2009, the two were back on the same side in the NBA All-Star Game. Combining for 44 points in the West's win over the East, the two players shared All-Star Game MVP honors.

Orlando easily won the deciding game in Boston, 101–82.

In the NBA finals, each of the first four games could have gone either way, but the Lakers emerged as winners in three of them. The most painful loss for Orlando came in Game 4, when they failed to secure victory at the free throw line late in the fourth quarter, and Los Angeles rallied to tie on Fisher's dramatic three-pointer (see pages 82–83). The Lakers went on to win 99–91 in overtime and deflate the Magic. Los Angeles won Game 5 in Orlando, 99–86.

WINNERS AND LEADERS

KING JAMES

In his sixth NBA season in 2008–09, Cleveland forward LeBron James earned his first NBA Most Valuable Player. James easily beat runner-up Kobe Bryant of the Los Angeles Lakers by getting 109 of a possible 121 first-place votes. James led the Cavaliers in scoring (28.4 points per game), rebounding (7.6), assists (7.2), and steals (1.7). More importantly, he led Cleveland to a league-best 66–16 record during the regular season. In the play-offs, the Cavaliers made it to the Eastern Conference finals before falling to the Orlando Magic.

2008–2009 NBA AWARD WINNERS

MOST VALUABLE PLAYER	**LeBron JAMES,** Cleveland
DEFENSIVE PLAYER OF THE YEAR	**Dwight HOWARD,** Orlando
ROOKIE OF THE YEAR	**Derrick ROSE,** Chicago
CITIZENSHIP AWARD	**Dikembe MUTOMBO**, Houston
SPORTSMANSHIP AWARD	**Chauncey BILLUPS,** Denver
SIXTH MAN AWARD	**Jason TERRY,** Dallas
MOST IMPROVED PLAYER	**Danny GRANGER,** Indiana
COACH OF THE YEAR	**Mike BROWN,** Cleveland

All-NBA

LeBron James was a unanimous choice for his second straight All-NBA team. Dwyane Wade made the top five for the first time after leading the league in scoring. Tim Duncan missed a First Team spot by only five votes!

FIRST TEAM	SECOND TEAM	THIRD TEAM
LeBron James, F, CLEVELAND	**Tim Duncan,** F, SAN ANTONIO	**Carmelo Anthony,** F, DENVER
Dirk Nowitzi, F, DALLAS	**Paul Pierce,** F, BOSTON	**Pau Gasol,** F, L.A. LAKERS
Dwight Howard, C, ORLANDO	**Yao Ming,** C, HOUSTON	**Shaquille O'Neal,** C, PHOENIX
Kobe Bryant, G, L.A. LAKERS	**Brandon Roy,** G, PORTLAND	**Chauncey Billups,** G, DENVER
Dwyane Wade, G, MIAMI	**Chris Paul,** G, NEW ORLEANS	**Tony Parker,** G, SAN ANTONIO

THE LEADERS

The top NBA performers in some key statistical categories for 2008–09:

CATEGORY	PLAYER, TEAM	MARK
SCORING	**Dwyane WADE,** Miami	**30.2** ▶
REBOUNDS	**Dwight HOWARD,** Orlando	**13.8**
◀ ASSISTS	**Chris PAUL,** New Orleans	**11.0**
◀ STEALS	**Chris PAUL,** New Orleans	**2.77**
BLOCKS	**Dwight HOWARD,** Orlando	**2.92**
FIELD-GOAL PCT.	**Shaquille O'NEAL,** Phoenix	**.609**
3-POINT FG PCT.	**Anthony MORROW,** Golden St.	**.467**
FREE-THROW PCT.	**Jose CALDERON,** Toronto	**.981**

BEHIND THE ARC

Derrick Rose

WHO'S NEXT?

Looking for the next wave of NBA stars? This All-Rookie team is a good place to start. Chicago guard Derrick Rose is at the head of that class after averaging 16.8 points and 6.3 assists while playing 37.0 minutes per game in his first season in the league. Rose was also named the league's Rookie of the Year. Next up are the NBA's 2009–2010 rookies, the first 10 picks of the 2009 NBA draft. It's a good bet that some of these names will make their way onto the All-Rookie team for 2009–10. After all, Rose was the top pick in 2008, out of the University of Memphis.

All-Rookie First Team

Derrick Rose, G, Chicago

O. J. Mayo, G, Memphis

Russell Westbrook, G, Oklahoma City

Brook Lopez, C, New Jersey

Michael Beasley, F, Miami

2009 NBA Draft (Picks 1–10)

NO.	NAME	POS.	NBA TEAM	COLLEGE/COUNTRY
1.	Blake GRIFFIN	F	L.A. Clippers	Oklahoma
2.	Hasheem THABEET	C	Memphis	Connecticut
3.	James HARDEN	G	Oklahoma City	Arizona State
4.	Tyreke EVANS	G	Sacramento	Memphis
5.	Ricky RUBIO	G	Minnesota	Spain
6.	Jonny FLYNN	G	Minnesota	Syracuse
7.	Stephen CURRY	G	Golden State	Davidson
8.	Jordan HILL	F	New York	Arizona
9.	DeMar DEROZAN	F	Toronto	So. California
10.	Brandon JENNINGS	G	Milwaukee	Italy

A LOOK AHEAD

Other Big Moves

Other teams tried to catch up to the Lakers by signing free agents or trading for new players. It was one of the biggest off-seasons ever for player movement. Lots of big names switched teams, including former Detroit forward/center Rasheed Wallace, who went to Boston. The Celtics, who won the NBA title in 2007–08, got burned when Kevin Garnett was injured and missed the 2008–09 playoffs. Wallace gives them more depth on the front line.

Also, Cleveland traded for center Shaquille O'Neal to take some of the heat off LeBron James. Can Shaq help James win his first title, just as he teamed with Kobe Bryant and Dwyane Wade in previous stops in his career?

Lakers Don't Stand Pat

Repeating as champions is one of the toughest feats in sports. Every team wants to knock off the champ, even if it's only for one night. The Lakers could have gone into the 2009–10 season with nearly the same team as their championship squad, and probably would have been the favorite to win it all again. Instead, they made a bold move to try to get even better by bringing in veteran forward Ron Artest while letting Trevor Ariza leave for Houston.

Tip-off in Taipei

The NBA continues to promote its game overseas, where it continues to gain in popularity. For the first time, a game was scheduled in Taipei, the capital city of Taiwan. The contest between the Denver Nuggets and the Indiana Pacers on October 8, 2009, was part of an international preseason schedule that also included games in England, Spain, and Mexico.

Artest picked 37 in honor of Michael Jackson.

The Detroit Shock pours onto the court to celebrate its return to the top of the WNBA.

WNBA SHOCK-ER!

After the Detroit Shock's disappointing finish to the 2007 season—they fell one game short of a WNBA championship—the team returned to the finals in 2008. This time, they left nothing to chance, sweeping the San Antonio Silver Stars in three games.

The championship was the Shock's third in a stretch of six years, and came in their fourth trip to the finals in that span. That puts them up there with the NBA's Detroit Pistons, who ruled their league in the late 1980s and early 1990s.

In fact, it is a former member of those Pistons teams, Shock coach and general manager Bill Laimbeer, who has helped take Detroit to the top. In 2002, Laimbeer took over as the coach of a team that had lost its first 10 games of the season. Laimbeer, who was a star center on the Pistons teams that won back-to-back NBA championships in 1988–89 and 1989–90, took the Shock to the WNBA finals by the next year. Detroit won the finals in 2003, then again in 2006. The Shock's 2006 title was the first of three straight trips to the finals.

In 2008, Detroit went 22–12 and won the WNBA East. They downed the Indiana Fever and the New York Liberty in the

> ***"Four trips to the finals in six years? That makes them one of the most successful sports franchises in any league in this decade."***
>
> — WNBA PRESIDENT DONNA ORENDER

Eastern Conference play-offs. In the West, San Antonio compiled a league-best 24–10 record, then beat the Sacramento Monarchs and the Los Angeles Sparks to reach the finals against Detroit.

While the Shock were old faces in the finals, the 2008 WNBA season also was notable for the number of new faces in the league. Several rookies played big roles, especially Candace Parker. The former Tennessee star was the two-time Wooden Award winner as the top college player. Joining the Los Angeles Sparks, Parker averaged 18.5 points and a league-best 9.5 rebounds per game while leading Los Angeles to within one second of reaching the WNBA finals.

Parker also made the highlight reels by becoming only the second player ever to dunk in a WNBA game. Chicago Sky center Sylvia Fowles didn't dunk, but she did get up high enough to become the first WNBA player to be whistled for goaltending. Despite suffering a knee injury on that play, she averaged 10.5 points and 7.5 rebounds per game as a rookie.

Several other first-year players in 2008 figure to be WNBA stars for years to come, too, including Minnesota guard Candice Wiggins, the league's Sixth Woman of the Year, and Detroit guard Alexis Hornbuckle, who led the league in steals while appearing in every game for the Shock.

Final 2008 Standings

EASTERN CONFERENCE	W	L	WESTERN CONFERENCE	W	L
Detroit	22	12	San Antonio	24	10
Connecticut	21	13	Seattle	22	12
New York	19	15	Los Angeles	20	14
Indiana	17	17	Sacramento	18	16
Chicago	12	22	Houston	17	17
Washington	10	24	Phoenix	16	18
Atlanta	4	30	Minnesota	16	18

Becky Hammon led San Antonio into the WNBA finals.

AROUND THE WNBA

Three's Company

Forward Candace Parker was the first overall pick of the 2008 WNBA draft and scored 34 points in her debut game for the Los Angeles Sparks . . . but she was just warming up. Parker was so good during her first pro season that she not only earned the WNBA's Rookie of the Year Award, but was also named the league's MVP. Only two other pro basketball players have done that: NBA Hall of Famers Wilt Chamberlain and Wes Unseld.

Parker got 2009 off to an even better start: In the spring, she gave birth to her first child, a baby girl. (Parker's husband is Shelden Williams, who plays for the NBA's Minnesota Timberwolves.) By early July, Candace was back on the basketball court.

Good as Gold

Even before the 2008 WNBA play-offs, Detroit Shock guard Katie Smith already had a pretty good year. A month earlier, she had played for the United States' gold-medal-winning team at the Olympics in Beijing. Then, after helping the Shock reach the WNBA finals with hard-fought victories over the Indiana Fever and the New York Liberty in the Eastern Conference play-offs, she really picked up her game in her team's three-game sweep of the San Antonio Silver Stars. Smith led the Shock in scoring in each of the wins and was named the finals MVP.

Shot of the Year

The Lakers' Derek Fisher made the NBA's shot of the year (see pages 82–83). San Antonio's Sophia Young got it for the WNBA with a thrilling buzzer-beater in Game 2 of the Western Conference finals against Los Angeles. The Sparks had won Game 1 and had a 66–65 lead with 1.3 seconds left in Game 2. Young took a pass from mid-court and nailed a 14-foot turnaround jumper as time ran out to give the Silver Stars a 67–66 victory. San Antonio then won Game 3 and the series.

STAT LEADERS

The top performers in some key WNBA statistical categories:

24.1 SCORING
Diana Taurasi, Phoenix

9.5 REBOUNDING
Candace Parker, Los Angeles

5.4 ASSISTS
Lindsay Whalen, Connecticut

2.32 STEALS
Alexis Hornbuckle, Detroit

2.94 BLOCKS
Lisa Leslie, Los Angeles

.546 FIELD-GOAL PCT.
Janel McCarville, New York

.45 3-POINT FG PCT.
Jamie Carey, Connecticut

.937 FREE-THROW PCT.
Becky Hammon, San Antonio

STAT STUFF

Six-time champ Michael Jordan

ALL-TIME NBA CHAMPS

Season	Champion
1946-47	**Philadelphia**
1947-48	**Baltimore**
1948-49	**Minneapolis**
1949-50	**Minneapolis**
1950-51	**Rochester**
1951-52	**Minneapolis**
1952-53	**Minneapolis**
1953-54	**Minneapolis**
1954-55	**Syracuse**
1955-56	**Philadelphia**
1956-57	**Boston**
1957-58	**St. Louis**
1958-59	**Boston**
1959-60	**Boston**
1960-61	**Boston**
1961-62	**Boston**
1962-63	**Boston**
1963-64	**Boston**
1964-65	**Boston**
1965-66	**Boston**
1966-67	**Philadelphia**
1967-68	**Boston**
1968-69	**Boston**
1969-70	**New York**
1970-71	**Milwaukee**
1971-72	**L.A. Lakers**
1972-73	**New York**
1973-74	**Boston**
1974-75	**Golden State**
1975-76	**Boston**
1976-77	**Portland**
1977-78	**Washington**
1978-79	**Seattle**
1979-80	**L.A. Lakers**
1980-81	**Boston**
1981-82	**L.A. Lakers**
1982-83	**Philadelphia**

1983-84	**Boston**
1984-85	**L.A. Lakers**
1985-86	**Boston**
1986-87	**L.A. Lakers**
1987-88	**L.A. Lakers**
1988-89	**Detroit**
1989-90	**Detroit**
1990-91	**Chicago**
1991-92	**Chicago**
1992-93	**Chicago**
1993-94	**Houston**
1994-95	**Houston**
1995-96	**Chicago**
1996-97	**Chicago**
1997-98	**Chicago**
1998-99	**San Antonio**
1999-00	**L.A. Lakers**
2000-01	**L.A. Lakers**
2001-02	**L.A. Lakers**
2002-03	**San Antonio**
2003-04	**Detroit**
2004-05	**San Antonio**
2005-06	**Miami**
2006-07	**San Antonio**
2007-08	**Boston**
2008-09	**L.A. Lakers**

ALL-TIME WNBA CHAMPS

1997	**Houston**
1998	**Houston**
1999	**Houston**
2000	**Houston**
2001	**Los Angeles**
2002	**Los Angeles**
2003	**Detroit**
2004	**Seattle**
2005	**Sacramento**
2006	**Detroit**
2007	**Phoenix**
2008	**Detroit**

Lisa Leslie was the MVP of the Sparks' 2002 WNBA title.

NHL

THE PUCK STOPS HERE!
Pittsburgh Penguins goaltender Marc-André Fleury protects the net during the Stanley Cup finals against the Detroit Red Wings. Fleury and his teammates thwarted the Red Wings' bid for a second consecutive title with a 2–1 victory in the deciding Game 7. It was Pittsburgh's first championship since 1991–92.

SEASON HIGHLIGHTS

When you think about penguins on ice, you might picture the lovable animals waddling around the Antarctic. But the big National Hockey League story in 2008–09 was about Penguins from Pittsburgh. The Penguins didn't waddle, but skated, to their first league title in 17 years, clinching the Stanley Cup in a hard-fought, seven-game series against the defending champions, the Detroit Red Wings.

There were plenty of other big stories in the NHL in 2008–09, too.

Montreal Canadiens' 100th Anniversary

The Canadiens are the most successful team in NHL history, with 24 Stanley Cup championships and the most famous players of all time. When the Canadiens opened the 2008–09 schedule against the Buffalo Sabres, they became the first pro hockey team to celebrate 100 seasons.

The Winter Classic

Hockey is a cold-weather sport, and there are few places colder than Chicago in January, so why not play hockey outside? Wrigley Field was the site of the NHL's annual Winter Classic, an outdoor match that has become one of hockey's most popular events. In the 2009 Classic, the Chicago Blackhawks and the Detroit Red Wings wore vintage sweaters and played a great game. The Red Wings won 6–4.

Bruins and Blackhawks Return to Glory

Hockey is an old sport, and its original six teams hold a special place in the hearts of all fans. Two of those teams, the Boston Bruins and the Chicago Blackhawks, had sensational seasons after many years of foundering. The Bruins, led by goaltender Tim Thomas, giant defenseman Zdeno Chara, and the terrific young power forward Milan Lucic, were at the top of the league standings for most of the year. The Blackhawks had two certified young superstars–Jonathan Toews and Patrick Kane–a Calder Trophy finalist (for best rookie) in Kris Versteeg, and a never-say-die team spirit that took them to the Stanley Cup semifinals.

Marty sets a record▼

New Jersey Devils goaltender Martin Brodeur missed most of the first half of the 2008–09 season with an injury, but came back with a special goal in sight: He was close to breaking the all-time wins record (551) of legendary Canadiens goaltender Patrick Roy. Brodeur tied the record in Montreal on March 14, with Roy on hand to congratulate him. He broke the record on March 17 in a 3–2 victory over the Blackhawks in New Jersey.

FINAL STANDINGS

EASTERN CONFERENCE	PTS
*__Boston__ Bruins	116
*__Washington__ Capitals	108
*__New Jersey__ Devils	106
Pittsburgh Penguins	99
Philadelphia Flyers	99
Carolina Hurricanes	97
New York Rangers	95
Montreal Canadiens	93
Florida Panthers	93
Buffalo Sabres	91
Ottawa Senators	83
Toronto Maple Leafs	81
Atlanta Thrashers	76
Tampa Bay Lightning	66
New York Islanders	61

WESTERN CONFERENCE	PTS
*__San Jose__ Sharks	117
*__Detroit__ Red Wings	112
*__Vancouver__ Canucks	100
Chicago Blackhawks	104
Calgary Flames	98
St. Louis Blues	92
Columbus Blue Jackets	92
Anaheim Mighty Ducks	91
Minnesota Wild	89
Nashville Predators	88
Edmonton Oilers	85
Dallas Stars	83
Phoenix Coyotes	79
Los Angeles Kings	79
Colorado Avalanche	69

*division winners

STANLEY CUP PLAY-OFFS

The Penguins winning the Stanley Cup was the biggest news of the play-offs, but there were other exciting stories, too. Led by their sensational rookie goalie, Steve Mason, the Columbus Blue Jackets made it to the play-offs for the first time in their nine-season history. The Blue Jackets played with a lot of heart but lost to the Detroit Red Wings, the defending champions, in the first round.

Both the St. Louis Blues and the Chicago Blackhawks returned to postseason play after many years of missing the play-offs. For the Blues it was five years, and for the Blackhawks it was seven. The Blues lost to the Vancouver Canucks in the first round, while the Blackhawks were knocked out in five games by the Red Wings in a fast-paced, thrill-packed Western Conference final series.

"I would've loved to do it in four [games]. It would have been a lot easier on the nerves." **– PENGUINS STAR MASON CROSBY, AFTER THE SEVEN-GAME FINAL**

The play-offs had big surprises. The San Jose Sharks chewed up the opposition all season and finished with the league's best record, but were sunk in the first round by the hard-hitting Anaheim Ducks. The Boston Bruins had the second-best record in the league, but were kicked out in the second round by the speedy Carolina Hurricanes.

The Stanley Cup finals pitted the Red Wings against the team they had beaten in the finals the year before, the Pittsburgh Penguins. The series began with two wins for the Red Wings on their home ice, with their tough forward Dan Cleary and rookie Justin Abdelkader scoring big goals, and with goaltender Chris Osgood playing brilliantly. When the series moved to Pittsburgh, the Penguins came to life. They won both home games, including a Game 4 third-period explosion in which they

The Ducks stunned the Sharks in the opening round.

The final series was close and exciting.

scored three goals in just 5 minutes and 37 seconds. The flurry included a goal by Sidney Crosby that turned out to be his only goal in the finals. When the series returned to Detroit, the Wings blew out the Penguins 5–0 for a three-games-to-two lead.

The teams returned to Pittsburgh, where the Penguins battled to a gritty 2–1 win in Game 6. In the Game 7 showdown in Detroit, Pittsburgh forward Maxime Talbot scored two goals–including a laser-beamed wrist shot over Osgood's shoulder. The Wings got one back and came within inches of tying the score when their captain, Nicklas Lidstrom, fired a point-blank shot that was stopped by goalie Marc-André Fleury in the final seconds. Fleury's save shut the door in Pittsburgh's 2–1 victory.

GAME 7 CLASSIC

The box score from the deciding game of the Stanley Cup Finals:

Pittsburgh	**0**	**2**	**0**	**—**	**2**
Detroit	**0**	**0**	**1**	**—**	**1**

Scoring: Talbot, Pit. (1:13, 2nd); Talbot, Pit. (10:07, 2nd); Ericsson, Det. (13:53, 3rd). **Shots on Goal:** Pit. 10-7-1–18; Det. 6-11-7–24

PLAY-OFF RESULTS

(Games won in parentheses)

FIRST ROUND

EASTERN CONFERENCE

Pittsburgh OVER **Philadelphia (4-2)**
Washington OVER **N.Y. Rangers (4-3)**
Carolina OVER **New Jersey (4-3)**
Boston OVER **Montreal (4-0)**

WESTERN CONFERENCE

Detroit OVER **Columbus (4-0)**
Anaheim OVER **San Jose (4-2)**
Chicago OVER **Calgary (4-2)**
Vancouver OVER **St. Louis (4-0)**

CONFERENCE SEMIFINALS

EASTERN CONFERENCE

Pittsburgh OVER **Washington (4-3)**
Carolina OVER **Boston (4-3)**

WESTERN CONFERENCE

Detroit OVER **Anaheim (4-3)**
Chicago OVER **Vancouver (4-2)**

CONFERENCE FINALS

EASTERN CONFERENCE

Pittsburgh OVER **Carolina (4-0)**

WESTERN CONFERENCE

Detroit OVER **Chicago (4-1)**

STANLEY CUP FINALS

Pittsburgh OVER **Detroit (4-3)**

2008–09 AWARDS

Stanley Cup
PITTSBURGH PENGUINS

Conn Smythe Trophy
(Stanley Cup Playoffs MVP)
EVGENI MALKIN, Pittsburgh Penguins

Clarence Campbell Bowl
(Western Conference Champions)
DETROIT RED WINGS

Prince of Wales Trophy
(Eastern Conference Champions)
PITTSBURGH PENGUINS

President's Trophy (League's Best Record)
SAN JOSE SHARKS

Hart Memorial Trophy (MVP)
◀◀◀ALEXANDER OVECHKIN,
Washington Capitals

Vezina Trophy (Best Goaltender)
TIM THOMAS, Boston Bruins

James Norris Memorial Trophy
(Best Defenseman)
ZDENO CHARA, Boston Bruins

Calder Memorial Trophy (Best Rookie)
STEVE MASON,
Columbus Blue Jackets

Frank J. Selke Trophy
(Best Defensive Forward)
PAVEL DATSYUK, Detroit Red Wings

Lady Byng Memorial Trophy
(Most Gentlemanly Player)
PAVEL DATSYUK, Detroit Red Wings

Jack Adams Award (Best Coach)
CLAUDE JULIEN, Boston Bruins

King Clancy Trophy
(Humanitarian Contribution to Hockey)
ETHAN MOREAU, Edmonton Oilers

Bill Masterton Memorial Trophy
(Perseverance, Sportsmanship, and Dedication to Hockey)
STEVE SULLIVAN, Nashville Predators

UP AHEAD ON THE ICE

◎ NHL IN EUROPE

The opening face-offs for the 2009–10 NHL season will take place October 2 and 3, 2009, in Scandinavia. The puck will drop in Stockholm, Sweden, when the Detroit Red Wings play two games against the St. Louis Blues. Helsinki, Finland, will host two games featuring the Chicago Blackhawks and the Florida Panthers.

◎ WINTER CLASSIC

Fenway Park in Boston, the home of baseball's Red Sox, is the place to be for hockey fans when the Boston Bruins face off against the Philadelphia Flyers in the NHL's popular Winter Classic on New Year's Day, 2010. These two top teams will battle it out with Fenway's legendary Green Monster (the left-field wall) looming over the rink.

◎ OLYMPICS

The NHL season will be put on hold for two weeks in February (and the All-Star game bypassed) when the international superstars of the league play for the glory of their homelands at the 2010 Winter Olympics in Vancouver. Team Canada will be going for the gold medal on its home ice, so that squad is the team to beat.

YOUNG STARS ON THE RISE

Jonathan TOEWS (Center, Chicago Blackhawks) The Blackhawks' captain is an excellent goal scorer (he was the top rookie goal scorer in 2007–08) and a fine defensive player. He led the Blackhawks on a thrilling play-off run in just his second season.

Jonas HILLER (Goaltender, Anaheim Ducks) The Swiss-born goaltender posted an impressive 2.06 goals against average in 23 regular-season games and dazzled in the play-offs with a 59-save outing in a Game 2 win over the Red Wings in the conference semifinals.

Nicklas BACKSTROM (Center, Washington Capitals) Alex Ovechkin scored 56 goals, and a lot of them came from assists by Backstrom. In addition to being one of the league's top set-up men, Backstrom can also put the puck in the net and do the hard work along the boards.

◂◂◂Milan LUCIC (Left Wing, Boston Bruins) In his second season, Milan Lucic has emerged as one of the league's best power forwards. Lucic has awesome size, pounds opponents with crunching body checks, and has tremendous offensive skills.

Ryan CALLAHAN (Left Wing, New York Rangers) Callahan scored 22 goals in 2008–09, but the feisty winger is at his best blocking shots and killing penalties.

STANLEY CUP CHAMPIONS

Season	Champion
2008–09	**Pittsburgh Penguins**
2007–08	**Detroit Red Wings**
2006–07	**Anaheim Ducks**
2005–06	**Carolina Hurricanes**
2004–05	No champion (Lockout)
2003–04	**Tampa Bay Lightning**
2002–03	**New Jersey Devils**
2001–02	**Detroit Red Wings**
2000–01	**Colorado Avalanche**
1999–00	**New Jersey Devils**
1998–99	**Dallas Stars**
1997–98	**Detroit Red Wings**
1996–97	**Detroit Red Wings**
1995–96	**Colorado Avalanche**
1994–95	**New Jersey Devils**
1993–94	**New York Rangers**
1992–93	**Montreal Canadiens**
1991–92	**Pittsburgh Penguins**
1990–91	**Pittsburgh Penguins**
1989–90	**Edmonton Oilers**
1988–89	**Calgary Flames**
1987–88	**Edmonton Oilers**
1986–87	**Edmonton Oilers**
1985–86	**Montreal Canadiens**
1984–85	**Edmonton Oilers**
1983–84	**Edmonton Oilers**
1982–83	**New York Islanders**
1981–82	**New York Islanders**
1980–81	**New York Islanders**
1979–80	**New York Islanders**
1978–79	**Montreal Canadiens**
1977–78	**Montreal Canadiens**
1976–77	**Montreal Canadiens**
1975–76	**Montreal Canadiens**
1974–75	**Philadelphia Flyers**
1973–74	**Philadelphia Flyers**
1972–73	**Montreal Canadiens**
1971–72	**Boston Bruins**
1970–71	**Montreal Canadiens**
1969–70	**Boston Bruins**
1968–69	**Montreal Canadiens**
1967–68	**Montreal Canadiens**
1966–67	**Toronto Maple Leafs**
1965–66	**Montreal Canadiens**
1964–65	**Montreal Canadiens**
1963–64	**Toronto Maple Leafs**
1962–63	**Toronto Maple Leafs**
1961–62	**Toronto Maple Leafs**
1960–61	**Chicago Blackhawks**
1959–60	**Montreal Canadiens**
1958–59	**Montreal Canadiens**
1957–58	**Montreal Canadiens**

1956–57	**Montreal Canadiens**
1955–56	**Montreal Canadiens**
1954–55	**Detroit Red Wings**
1953–54	**Detroit Red Wings**
1952–53	**Montreal Canadiens**
1951–52	**Detroit Red Wings**
1950–51	**Toronto Maple Leafs**
1949–50	**Detroit Red Wings**
1948–49	**Toronto Maple Leafs**
1947–48	**Toronto Maple Leafs**
1946–47	**Toronto Maple Leafs**
1945–46	**Montreal Canadiens**
1944–45	**Toronto Maple Leafs**
1943–44	**Montreal Canadiens**
1942–43	**Detroit Red Wings**
1941–42	**Toronto Maple Leafs**
1940–41	**Boston Bruins**
1939–40	**New York Rangers**
1938–39	**Boston Bruins**
1937–38	**Chicago Blackhawks**
1936–37	**Detroit Red Wings**
1935–36	**Detroit Red Wings**
1934–35	**Montreal Maroons**
1933–34	**Chicago Blackhawks**
1932–33	**New York Rangers**
1931–32	**Toronto Maple Leafs**
1930–31	**Montreal Canadiens**
1929–30	**Montreal Canadiens**
1928–29	**Boston Bruins**

Canadiens captain Butch Bouchard (1955–56)

1927–28	**New York Rangers**
1926–27	**Ottawa Senators**
1925–26	**Montreal Maroons**
1924–25	**Victoria Cougars**
1923–24	**Montreal Canadiens**
1922–23	**Ottawa Senators**
1921–22	**Toronto St. Pats**
1920–21	**Ottawa Senators**
1919–20	**Ottawa Senators**
1918–19	No decision
1917–18	**Toronto Arenas**
1916–17	**Seattle Metropolitans**
1915–16	**Montreal Canadiens**
1914–15	**Vancouver Millionaires**
1913–14	**Toronto Blueshirts**
1912–13	**Quebec Bulldogs**
1911–12	**Quebec Bulldogs**
1910–11	**Ottawa Senators**

48

JIMMIE GOES FOR THREE!
Jimmie Johnson became the first driver since 1978 to win three straight NASCAR championships. Smart, steady, and super-talented, Johnson has become the national face of America's most popular motor sport.

JIMMIE DOES IT AGAIN!

With two straight NASCAR titles heading into 2008, Jimmie Johnson rolled toward a rare "threepeat." Having earned four wins and nine top 5s through the first 26 races, Johnson was in prime position when The Chase for the Cup started with race No. 27. However, his opponents were going to make it tough.

Amid all the excitement over Johnson's drive for three, a guy who didn't get as much run was Kyle Busch. Competing in Nationwide, Craftsman Truck (see pages 112–113), and Sprint Cup races, Busch had won 21 races overall. Thanks to eight of those wins, Busch held the lead as The Chase began. Carl Edwards was also hot with a season-high nine wins, and would become Johnson's biggest rival for the title.

Jimmie Johnson with the 2008 trophy.

FAST FACT: South Carolina superstar driver **CALE YARBOROUGH** was the first driver to win three straight NASCAR championships. He put together his streak in 1976, 1977, and 1978, while driving a familiar No. 11 orange and gold Chevy.

However, once The Chase began, Johnson kicked his No. 48 car team into high gear. They won three of the final 12 races and finished in the top five in three others. This steady excellence helped hold off Carl Edwards for the record-tying third straight championship.

There was plenty NASCAR racing action on the way to that exciting finish. The season kicked off with a classic Daytona 500. Ryan Newman won, but it took some fancy driving on the last laps for him to hold off Tony Stewart. Stewart himself was a big story by midsummer. He announced that, in 2009,

> ***"Jimmie has the ability to handle multiple thoughts at the same time like no one else in NASCAR. Another big reason he's been successful—he's a genuinely nice guy."***
>
> — JACK STARK, SPORTS PSYCHOLOGIST

Can Johnson become the first to go four in a row in 2009? It'll be quite a race!

he would own his own racing team. He left behind longtime team owner Joe Gibbs to strike out as a rare owner-driver. In June 2009, Tony became the first owner-driver in 10 years to win a race!

Meanwhile, another hot driver made things a little hotter by continuing a feud with Kyle Busch. Carl Edwards, famous for doing a backflip from his car after his steadily-mounting series of race wins, dueled often with Busch. It came to a head at a race in Bristol in August. After Edwards used a little bump to pass Busch, heated words were exchanged. The duels on and off the track between these two great drivers will be fun for fans to watch in the coming years.

Jeff Gordon stunned many by going without a victory for the first time in 14 years. (However, he started off in 2009 with two wins in the first 10 weeks.) Dale Earnhardt Jr., with the Hendricks team, struggled but still managed to please his fans by making The Chase. NASCAR itself battled a bit in 2008 and 2009, as some fans had trouble affording tickets and trips. However, the coming seasons look like racing fun for everyone!

CHASE FOR THE CUP

2008 FINAL STANDINGS

PLACE/DRIVER	POINTS
1. **Jimmie JOHNSON**	6684
2. **Carl EDWARDS**	6615
3. **Greg BIFFLE**	6467
4. **Kevin HARVICK**	6408
5. **Clint BOWYER**	6381
6. **Jeff BURTON**	6335
7. **Jeff GORDON**	6316
8. **Denny HAMLIN**	6214
9. **Tony STEWART**	6202
10. **Kyle BUSCH**	6186
11. **Matt KENSETH**	6184
12. **Dale EARNHARDT Jr.**	6127

MEET THE DRIVERS!

JIMMIE **JOHNSON**

Jimmie got his racing start in the desert. Johnson was a star in the rough-and-tumble world of off-road desert racing. He also raced trucks in stadiums on hilly, bouncy, rugged dirt tracks. But he made the jump to stock cars and soon used the skills he learned in the desert on the hard tracks of NASCAR. He won three races in his first full season in 2002 . . . and hasn't won less in a season since! He even has a pair of second-place season results to to go with his amazing three NASCAR championships.

CARL **EDWARDS**

Fans have flipped for this energetic racer as he has charged up the standings in the past two seasons. Edwards won four races in his first season, but then struggled in 2006 with no wins. Two years later, he had a season-high nine wins in 2008. After every win, he stands on the window frame of his car and then does a backflip onto the infield!

KYLE **BUSCH**

Is this young driver the next big NASCAR superstar? Following in his brother Kurt's tire tracks, Kyle's skills have put him among the best in the sport. He has won at least one race in each of his five full seasons. He won his first race when he was only 20! In 2008, he had his best season yet, winning eight Sprint Cup races.

Nationwide Series Report

Clint Bowyer led for nearly two-thirds of the year on the way to his first Nationwide championship. (This was the first season the series ran under its new name, taking over from the long-running Busch Series.) Though he finished sixth overall, Kyle Busch had an amazing season, winning 10 races. The big news for Nationwide in 2009 was the introduction of its own version of the Car of Tomorrow. The Sprint Cup level has been using the COT for two seasons. How will it affect Nationwide teams and drivers? All the testing time and the experience of Sprint Cup should make the transition a smooth one.

LADY IS A CHAMP

Pit crews normally work in the shadow of their famous drivers. For the annual Pit Crew Challenge, they take centerstage. Crews match their skills at tire-changing, fueling, and pushing the car. In May 2009, the crew of Jeff Burton's No. 31 car pulled a fast one–literally. They put the 100-pound Kim Burton, Jeff's wife, behind the wheel. The weight savings helped them shave precious time on their way to capturing the championship!

CRAFTSMAN TRUCK SERIES REPORT

Johnny Benson *just* slipped into first place ahead of veteran truck racer Ron Hornaday. Benson's seven-point victory was the second-closest in series history. He finished seventh in the final race, just four truck lengths ahead of Hornaday, to clinch the title. For 2009, the series name changed to Camping World.

AROUND THE TRACK

"Tire"d in Indy ▲

By using a new type of tires, NASCAR tried to fix a problem with tires on the hard, flat track at the Indianapolis Motor Speedway. Turns out they made it worse. Every team struggled with blown and worn tires at the 2008 Brickyard 400. Jimmie Johnson's fast pit crew made the difference in winning the race.

Biffle's Back ▶

A few years ago, Greg Biffle was the "next big thing." But he struggled for several seasons, missing The Chase for the Cup. That ended in 2008. He had a solid season even though he didn't win a race. However, in The Chase for the Cup, he won the first two races and ended up finishing third overall.

Finally on Father's Day

Dale Earnhardt Jr. had not won in 75 straight races through the middle of 2008. Finally, in an exciting duel in Michigan on Father's Day, he snapped the streak and thrilled his many fans.

Kasey at the Bat

Fans voted Kasey Kahne into the 2008 All-Star Race at the last moment. He responded by winning from a last-place start. Fans later voted the win the biggest moment in the long history of the Lowe's Motor Speedway.

Can't Get Much Closer ▲

Erik Darnell held off Johnny Benson to win a Craftsman Truck Series race in Michigan. No big deal, right? Wrong! Darnell won by 0.005 seconds! It was the closest finish ever in NASCAR history!

Way to Go, Kid!

In a race at Kentucky, Joey Logano became the youngest winner in Nationwide Series history. His win, and four other top-fives, left him No. 20 overall in the series.

Tony the Tiger! ▶

At Pocono in June 2009, Tony Stewart became the first owner-driver in more than 11 years to win a NASCAR race. Tony left the Joe Gibbs team for 2009, striking out on his own as a team owner. He still has plenty of skill behind the wheel, though, and was leading the NASCAR season points standings after the race. Tony had also won the non-points Sprint All-Star Race a few weeks earlier.

UP, UP, AND AWAY

In the Aaron's 499 at Talladega in April 2009, some fans got a little too close to the action. Late in the race, Carl Edwards was trying to pass young Brad Keselowski (who ended up winning) on the final lap. A bump, a spin, and a moment later, Edwards was airborne! His car flew toward the huge fence that protects the fans. The fence caught his car like a catcher's mitt and it landed back on the track. Edwards was okay, but several fans were injured by flying debris.

LUG NUTS

NEWS AND NOTES FROM NASCAR 2009

* One NASCAR fan was literally out of this world. In July, U.S. astronaut Doug Hurley piloted the space shuttle Endeavour into space (going much faster than a NASCAR driver, by the way). For his moments of relaxation in orbit, he brought along a DVD of NASCAR highlights so he could watch his driving heroes circle the track while he circled the Earth!

◄◄◄ * In August, Jimmie Johnson led a group of NASCAR drivers and officials to the White House to meet President Barack Obama.

* Veteran driver Mark Martin almost retired a couple of years ago. He's glad he stuck around. He won 4 races in 2009 and started his 1,000th career race, becoming only the third driver to reach that total. He also became only the fourth driver older than 50 years old to win a Sprint Cup race and the oldest ever to lead the points standings, which he did briefly early in the season.

LOOKING AHEAD

WHO'S NEXT? You know all the current superstar racers. But who will be the next drivers to emerge from the younger ranks and compete for the top spot? Here's a look at some up-and-coming drivers:

Joey LOGANO: In 2008, Joey became one of the youngest NASCAR drivers ever, making his first ride at the age of only 18. He'll add experience to his skills and be a driver to watch.

David RAGAN: His 2008 season was just his second on the circuit, but he missed The Chase for the Cup by just one place.

Regan SMITH: The 2008 Rookie of the Year, he was the first rookie driver to finish every race he started! Steady performances like that mean a bright future for this New Yorker.

2009 NASCAR CHAMPION

Well, we had to print this book before the final races of The 2009 Chase for the Cup. So we can't tell you who won . . . but we can guess. Based on our NASCAR knowledge, we predict that the 2009 Chase for the Cup champ will be (envelope, please):

★Jeff Gordon★

We think the four-time champ will return to the top and prevent Johnson from a fourth straight title.

ALL-TIME NASCAR CHAMPIONS

2008	Jimmie Johnson	Chevrolet
2007	Jimmie Johnson	Chevrolet
2006	Jimmie Johnson	Chevrolet
2005	Tony Stewart	Chevrolet
2004	Kurt Busch	Ford
2003	Matt Kenseth	Ford
2002	Tony Stewart	Pontiac
2001	Jeff Gordon	Chevrolet
2000	Bobby Labonte	Pontiac
1999	Dale Jarrett	Ford
1998	Jeff Gordon	Chevrolet
1997	Jeff Gordon	Chevrolet
1996	Terry Labonte	Chevrolet
1995	Jeff Gordon	Chevrolet
1994	Dale Earnhardt	Chevrolet
1993	Dale Earnhardt	Chevrolet
1992	Alan Kulwicki	Ford
1991	Dale Earnhardt	Chevrolet
1990	Dale Earnhardt	Chevrolet
1989	Rusty Wallace	Pontiac
1988	Bill Elliott	Ford
1987	Dale Earnhardt	Chevrolet
1986	Dale Earnhardt	Chevrolet
1985	Darrell Waltrip	Chevrolet
1984	Terry Labonte	Chevrolet
1983	Bobby Allison	Buick
1982	Darrell Waltrip	Buick
1981	Darrell Waltrip	Buick
1980	Dale Earnhardt	Chevrolet
1979	Richard Petty	Chevrolet
1978	Cale Yarborough	Oldsmobile
1977	Cale Yarborough	Chevrolet
1976	Cale Yarborough	Chevrolet
1975	Richard Petty	Dodge
1974	Richard Petty	Dodge
1973	Benny Parsons	Chevrolet
1972	Richard Petty	Plymouth
1971	Richard Petty	Plymouth

"One of these days, they'll hold a NASCAR race and I won't show up. That's when they'll know I'm retired."

— SEVEN-TIME NASCAR CHAMPION RICHARD PETTY, STILL AN ACTIVE CAR OWNER, ON WHETHER HE'LL EVER LEAVE THE SPORT HE LOVES

1970	Bobby Isaac	Dodge
1969	David Pearson	Ford
1968	David Pearson	Ford
1967	Richard Petty	Plymouth
1966	David Pearson	Dodge
1965	Ned Jarrett	Ford
1964	Richard Petty	Plymouth
1963	Joe Weatherly	Pontiac
1962	Joe Weatherly	Pontiac
1961	Ned Jarrett	Chevrolet
1960	Rex White	Chevrolet
1959	Lee Petty	Plymouth
1958	Lee Petty	Oldsmobile
1957	Buck Baker	Chevrolet
1956	Buck Baker	Chrysler
1955	Tim Flock	Chrysler
1954	Lee Petty	Chrysler
1953	Herb Thomas	Hudson
1952	Tim Flock	Hudson
1951	Herb Thomas	Hudson
1950	Bill Rexford	Oldsmobile
1949	Red Byron	Oldsmobile

OTHER MOTOR SPORTS

START YOUR ENGINES!

It's all about speed! Here's Top Fuel dragster driver Tony Schumacher about to hurtle more than 300 miles per hour down the track. He's competing in the SummitRacing.com Nationals in Las Vegas, Nevada, in August of 2008. Tony was just about a "Schu-in" to win any race he entered in his record-breaking 2008 season

2008 NHRA CHAMPIONS

The Checkered Flag Goes to . . .

Tony Schumacher. And Cruz Pedregon. And Jeg Coughlin. They were the winners of the three top classes of professional drag racing sanctioned by the National Hot Rod Association (NHRA) in 2008: Top Fuel (Schumacher), Funny Cars (Pedregon), and Pro Stock (Coughlin).

Record Run

Tony Schumacher had one of the greatest seasons in drag-racing history. He won a record 15 of the 24 Top Fuel events in 2008, including seven in a row in one stretch (another record). By the end of the season, he easily outdistanced the competition for his fifth season title in a row, and the sixth of his career. He also upped his career victory total to 56 events. You guessed it: Those are all records, too!

New for 2009

For the first time, Top Fuel and Funny Cars were scheduled to run a full season's worth of races at only 1,000 feet. Traditionally, the standard distance of a drag race has been one quarter of a mile. That's 1,320 feet. But shortly after the death of popular driver Scott Kalitta in a Funny Car race in June of 2008, NHRA shortened the races in the two categories with the most powerful engines.

◂◂Ladies' Days

Drag racing is one of the few sports in which women pros compete on the same field as the men. Several of those ladies had big days in 2008. At Atlanta

Cruz Pedregon was the Funny Car champ.

in April, Ashley Force became the first woman to win a Funny Car event. Several weeks later in Bristol, Tennessee, Melanie Troxel became the second. Hillary Will also broke into the winner's circle in a Top Fuel event in Topeka, Kansas.

ALL IN THE FAMILY

Cruz Pedregon won the Funny Car championship for 2008 with a little help from his younger brother, Tony Pedregon. Cruz entered the final event of the season in first place, with Robert Hight in close pursuit. But when Tony beat Hight in the opening round of the Southern California Nationals in Pomona, Cruz clinched the title. Cruz also had been the champ back in 1992; Tony won in 2003.

SEASON STANDINGS

TOP FUEL

	DRIVER	POINTS
1.	Tony SCHUMACHER	2703
2.	Larry DIXON	2445
3.	Cory McCLENATHAN	2406
4.	Hillary WILL	2405
5.	Antron BROWN	2370

FUNNY CAR

	DRIVER	POINTS
1.	Cruz PEDREGON	2561
2.	Tim WILKERSON	2468
3.	Jack BECKMAN	2457
4.	Robert HIGHT	2442
5.	Tony PEDREGON	2440

PRO STOCK

	DRIVER	POINTS
1.	Jeg COUGHLIN	2523
2.	Greg ANDERSON	2487
3.	Kurt JOHNSON	2450
4t.	Mike EDWARDS	2388
4t.	Jason LINE	2388

FORMULA 1

"Getting married, winning a 500, winning a championship in one year—not too many people can probably say they've done that." — LEWIS HAMILTON

The Checkered Flag Goes to . . .

Lewis Hamilton. In a thrilling season chase, Hamilton beat runner-up Felipe Massa by just one point to win the Formula 1 World Driving Championship for 2008. It was the second year in a row that the title was decided by just a single point. In 2007, Hamilton missed out by that margin when Kimi Raikkonen won the last race of the season.

Missions Accomplished

Lewis Hamilton's Formula 1 world championship in 2008 was big for several reasons. He was the first British driver to win the title since Damon Hill in 1996. He was the first black driver ever to win it. And, at 23 years old, he was also the youngest driver ever to be the season champion.

Road Trip

When they call the winner of the Formula 1 season points title the "world champion," they really mean it! F1 grand prix events are held all over the world, including places such as Malaysia, Bahrain, Spain, Turkey, Hungary, Italy, Japan, and China. Strangely, though, there were no races scheduled for the

New for 2009

Slick tires weren't really new to Formula 1 racing for 2009, they just made a comeback. From 1998 to 2008, Formula 1 cars used grooved tires. Slick tires, or "racing slicks," returned in 2009. Racing slicks have no grooves. That means more of the tire grips the road, for better traction and handling in dry weather. Slick tires are not appropriate for regular passenger vehicles, which need grooves in the tread to help displace water in wet conditions.

United States or Canada in 2009. That marked the first time there were no races in North America in the 60-season history of F1 championship events.

Old Enough to Drive

Speaking of young drivers, Sebastian Vettel became the youngest driver ever to win a Formula 1 grand prix event. A German, Vettel won the Italian Grand Prix in Monza in September of 2008. Vettel was less than three months past his 21st birthday. "For sure, the best day of my life," he said.

That's Vettel with a "V"—as in victory.

SEASON STANDINGS

DRIVER	POINTS
1. LEWIS HAMILTON	98
2. FELIPE MASSA	97
3T. KIMI RAIKKONEN	75
3T. ROBERT KUBICA	75
5. FERNANDO ALONSO	61

Indy car champ Scott Dixon is pictured in a familiar spot—ahead of the rest of the field.

INDYCAR

The Checkered Flag Goes to . . . Scott Dixon. He beat second-place Helio Castroneves by 17 points to win his second Indy Racing League (IRL) season championship in 2008, and his first since his rookie season in 2003. Dixon equaled an IRL record by winning six races, including the biggest race on the series schedule: the Indianapolis 500.

Good News for Helio? Scott Dixon's championship in 2008 marked the fourth year in a row that the winner of the prestigious Indianapolis 500 went on to win the season points title, too. Helio Castroneves hoped that trend would continue for 2009. In May that year, Helio won at Indy for the third time in his career. He held off Dan Wheldon (who won the race in 2005) by nearly two seconds.

More Than Just a Pretty Face

Danica Patrick first made a name for herself on the IRL circuit for her good looks. And in her brief career (she was a rookie in 2005), she's become the most visible face in Indy car racing–and maybe all of motor sports. All the attention is warranted, though. Danica finished sixth in the season standings in 2008, the year that she became the first woman to win an IRL race (the Twin Ring Motegi in Japan). The next May, she finished third at the Indianapolis 500–the highest finish ever in that race by a female driver.

All for One and One for All

For the first time since 1995, the year before the IRL's first season, IndyCar racing featured a unified series in 2008. The IRL and the Champ Car World Series (CCWS) made peace before the start of the season.

WILL SHE OR WON'T SHE?

As the 2009 season went on, rumors continued that Danica Patrick would make the jump from IndyCar racing to NASCAR. True, such rumors came and went just about every year. But with only NASCAR drivers Jeff Gordon and Dale Earnhardt Jr. rivaling Danica's name recognition among race-car stars, and with her contract with Andretti Green Racing completed at the end of the year, many experts speculated that the time was right. A report in September that Patrick would drive in Nationwide and Truck Series races for Tony Stewart's team was not confirmed, but it would be a good first step.

Game of Inches

The 2008 season ended when Helio Castroneves edged Scott Dixon by only inches in a race at the Chicagoland Speedway. Castroneves's winning time was .0033 seconds (that's just over three one-thousandths of one second) better than Dixon's time. Don't feel bad for Dixon, though. He still earned enough points to clinch the season championship. Oh, yeah, and the $1 million bonus prize that goes with it.

Season Standings

DRIVER	POINTS
1. Scott Dixon	646
2. Helio Castroneves	629
3. Tony Kanaan	513
4. Dan Wheldon	492
5. Ryan Briscoe	447

MOTOCROSS/SUPERCROSS

The Checkered Flag Goes to . . .

James Stewart Jr., or "Bubba," as he is commonly known, won his first American Motorcyclist Association (AMA) championship in the Motocross class (250-cc bikes) in 2008. The rider once called the "Tiger Woods of motocross" also won the AMA Supercross championship in 2009 for the second time in three years (the short season ends in May). Chad Reed won that title in 2008.

"The day was pretty nerve-wracking for me. . . . A lot of emotions, a lot of tears went into this." — JAMES "BUBBA" STEWART, on the day that he won the AMA Supercross championship for 2009

Champion Lite

Ryan Villopoto has become the dominant rider in the "Lites" class (125-cc bikes) of motocross racing. In 2008, he won his third consecutive AMA championship in that class. A highly touted amateur star in the early 2000s, he turned professional in 2005 and won his first AMA season title the next year.

Double-Double

Australian Cam Sinclair became the first rider to perform a double backflip in freestyle competition–and he did it twice at the Red Bull X-Fighters World Tour stop in Fort Worth, Texas, in June of 2009. (Double backflips had been done before in events such as the Best Trick competition at the X Games, but never in freestyle, which is a timed event with multiple ramps and tricks.) Believe it or not, Sinclair didn't win the competition. His feats rattled his bones so much that he had to pull out before the final. American Nate Adams won.

EVERYTHING ON WHEELS (AND MORE!)

There are motor sports for just about anything on wheels. Trucks, monster trucks, sprint cars, midget cars, and on and on–way too many to list here.

▲✸ Pro Stock Motorcycles are a popular segment of drag racing. Eddie Krawiec was the '08 champ.

✸ Would you believe there's even a United States Lawn Mower Association (USLMA)? Jim Mikula of Michigan was the driver of the year for 2008. ▶

They race things that don't even have wheels, too:

✸ The World Championship Snowmobile Derby is held each January in Eagle River, Wisconsin. Brian Bewcyk won the event in 2008 and 2009. In powerboat racing, American Jay Price was the world champion for 2008.

MAJOR CHAMPIONS OF THE 2000s

TOP FUEL DRAGSTERS

YEAR	DRIVER
2000	Gary Scelzi
2001	Kenny Bernstein
2002	Larry Dixon
2003	Larry Dixon
2004	Tony Schumacher
2005	Tony Schumacher
2006	Tony Schumacher
2007	Tony Schumacher
2008	Tony Schumacher

John Force is a Funny Car legend.

FUNNY CARS

YEAR	DRIVER
2000	John Force
2001	John Force
2002	John Force
2003	Tony Pedregon
2004	John Force
2005	Gary Scelzi
2006	John Force
2007	Tony Pedregon
2008	Cruz Pedregon

PRO STOCK CARS

YEAR	DRIVER
2000	Jeg Coughlin Jr.
2001	Warren Johnson
2002	Jeg Coughlin Jr.
2003	Greg Anderson
2004	Greg Anderson
2005	Greg Anderson
2006	Jason Line
2007	Jeg Coughlin Jr.
2008	Jeg Coughlin Jr.

FORMULA 1

YEAR	DRIVER
2000	Michael Schumacher
2001	Michael Schumacher
2002	Michael Schumacher
2003	Michael Schumacher
2004	Michael Schumacher
2005	Fernando Alonso
2006	Fernando Alonso

Dan Wheldon zooms around a turn.

2007	Kimi Raikkonen
2008	Lewis Hamilton

INDY RACING LEAGUE

YEAR	DRIVER
2000	Buddy Lazier
2001	Sam Hornish Jr.
2002	Sam Hornish Jr.
2003	Scott Dixon
2004	Tony Kanaan
2005	Dan Wheldon
2006	Sam Hornish Jr. and Dan Wheldon (tie)
2007	Dario Franchitti
2008	Scott Dixon

AMA SUPERCROSS

YEAR	DRIVER
2000	Jeremy McGrath
2001	Ricky Carmichael
2002	Ricky Carmichael
2003	Ricky Carmichael
2004	Chad Reed
2005	Ricky Carmichael
2006	Ricky Carmichael
2007	James Stewart Jr.
2008	Chad Reed
2009	James Stewart Jr.

AMA MOTOCROSS

YEAR	RIDER (MOTOCROSS)	RIDER (LITES)
2000	Ricky Carmichael	Travis Pastrana
2001	Ricky Carmichael	Mike Brown
2002	Ricky Carmichael	James Stewart Jr.
2003	Ricky Carmichael	Grant Langston
2004	Ricky Carmichael	James Stewart Jr.
2005	Ricky Carmichael	Ivan Tedesco
2006	Ricky Carmichael	Ryan Villopoto
2007	Grant Langston	Ryan Villopoto
2008	James Stewart Jr.	Ryan Villopoto

Ricky Carmichael

FLYING HIGH

Now that's some big air! Shaun White appears to soar above the trees as he competes in the finals of the snowboard slopestyle at the Winter X Games in Aspen, Colorado, in January of 2009. White's clutch performance on his final run earned him the gold medal.

What goes up must come down! Robbie Maddison returns to street level after his big jump.

2008–2009 WRAP-UP

Australian Robbie Maddison started off the 2009 action sports year with a bang, leaping nearly 100 feet on his motorbike to the top of the Arc de Triomphe monument late on New Year's Eve. Okay, it wasn't the real Arc de Triomphe. It was the replica of the famous French landmark that stands among the luxury hotels in Las Vegas, Nevada. But it was a real 100 feet (actually, 96 feet, or 29.26 meters). And after Maddison soared to the top, what was left to do? Come down, of course! He sailed freefall more than 60 feet through the air, landing on a ramp with a jarring thud that brought him back to a roaring crowd of onlookers cheering him from the city streets.

Maddison's insane jump was the kind of push-the-envelope stunt that sets action sports apart from other sports. (Warning! Action sports stars are professionals who have many years of experience and proper training, and use the latest safety equipment. In other words, don't try these kinds of stunts!) The rest of the action sports year featured a blend of recognizable pros and, of course, rising young stars.

The usual list of veterans included the likes of surfer Kelly Slater and skateboarder/snowboarder Shaun White. Those athletes are known even to folks who aren't huge fans of action sports because of their commercial tie-ins and product endorsements. After a one-year absence from the top, Slater bounced back in 2008 to win his ninth Association of Surfing Professionals (ASP) world title. White, meanwhile, won his record eighth and ninth X Games gold medals in January of 2009 at the Winter X Games 13.

Here are some other notable action sports achievements from 2008–09:

- Phillip Soven, age 19, won his second consecutive Pro Wakeboard Tour championship in 2008.
- After near misses in 2005 and 2007, Canadian Pierre-Luc Gagnon won the AST Dew Tour skateboard vert title for 2008. Chaz Ortiz ended Ryan Sheckler's three-year run atop the skate park standings.
- Other AST Dew Tour winners for 2008 included Jamie Bestwick (BMX vert), Daniel Dhers (BMX park), Cameron White (BMX dirt), and Adam Jones (FMX).

Skateboard champ Pierre-Luc Gagnon looks like he can defy gravity.

- In women's surfing, Stephanie Gilmore won the ASP world title for the second year in a row in 2008. Gilmore, who was just 19 years old when she debuted in 2007, proved that her big rookie season was no fluke. She entered 2009 as the top-rated women's surfer.
- On the men's side of surfing, after Slater dominated the schedule to win the world title in 2008, Australia's Joel Parkinson got off to a hot start in 2009 and took over the top spot in the ratings early in the season.

Kelly Slater can ride the waves better than just about any other surfer ever.

WINTER X GAMES

So Close!

Dane Ferguson won the gold medal in the snowmobile next trick, but it was a failed attempt by Levi LaVallee that had everyone talking. LaVallee remembered watching his friend Travis Pastrana do a double backflip on his bike at the Summer X Games in 2006. "How cool would that be to do on a snowmobile?" LaVallee thought. Never mind that his 450-pound snowmobile was twice the weight of Pastrana's bike! LaVallee tried the stunt at Winter X Games 13 and actually pulled off the jump, but couldn't stick the landing. The force of it jarred him off his snowmobile, and the rules say he's got to stay on the vehicle. So the trick didn't count in the scoring . . . but it still made all the highlight reels!

No Hotdogging

Lindsey Jacobellis is a perennial gold medalist in the women's snowboarder X, although a lot of casual sports fans know her because she lost a gold medal at the 2006 Winter Olympics when she fell while hotdogging near the finish line. She didn't take any chances at Winter X Games 13, speeding across the finish line even though she had left the rest of the field 25 yards behind. Nate Holland's victory on the men's side of snowboarder X was a lot closer. Late in the finals, he made a cool move by ducking down inside of leader Stian Sivertzen to get ahead. After Sivertzen stumbled a moment later, Holland went on to take his fourth consecutive gold medal in the event.

Board Champ

No X Games report would be complete without Shaun White. The most famous snowboarder of all time was a big factor, as usual, in Aspen in 2009, when he picked up the record eighth and ninth gold medals of his career. White's victory in the slopestyle was not without controversy, as some analysts were surprised that his solid final run was enough to overtake silver medalist Kevin Pearce. White left no doubt in the superpipe, however, when his final run vaulted him to the top.

"I've had a couple of mistakes in the past season or so, and that's driving me to do well. . . . I want to get back on top."

— SHAUN WHITE, BEFORE WINTER X GAMES 13

This photograph catches Levi LaVallee and his snowmobile in the middle of a double backflip.

Surprise Winner

Americans Tanner Hall (the X Games winner in 2006, 2007, and 2008) and Simon Dumont (2004 and 2005) had dominated the men's skiing superpipe in recent years, but France's Xavier Bertoni was the upset winner in 2009. Bertoni made all the tough jumps look easy en route to his first gold medal. Hall was second and Dumont was third.

Other notable performances from Winter X Games 13:

◀◀◀ ◎ Australian Torah Bright was second in the women's superpipe snowboarding in 2006, then first in 2007, then second in 2008. So 2009 was her year to finish back on top, which she did.

◎ The United States' Tucker Hibbert wins the snowmobile snocross every year—or so it seems. Hibbert's victory in 2009 marked his third in a row and fourth overall. (He also has two silver medals in the 12-year history of the event.)

◎ Canada's Sarah Burke won the women's skiing

SUMMER X GAMES

Where There's a Will There's a Way

Danny Way gets injured . . . looks as if he can't go on . . . gets up against overwhelming odds . . . wins gold medal. Repeat. That's been the story line of the most recent X Games. It happened at Summer X Games 15 in Los Angeles in 2009–just as it did at X Games 14 in 2008. Way, the "King of Big Air," won his signature skateboard event in 2008 after a couple of scary crashes. In '09, he decided to forgo big air to concentrate on rail jam. An injury in practice left him hobbling on crutches the day of the event, but he tossed those aside. Then he turned an ankle after hitting the rail on his second run. After limping off, he came back to nail a switch trick for the gold medal.

"I don't know why I always have to be the guy that has to get hurt and prove you can keep going. I don't know if I like that title very much." — DANNY WAY

Way came back from this scary crash.

Crossover Appeal

Perhaps the biggest news of X Games 15 was a stunt in the moto best trick competition that failed. Travis Pastrana created a lot of buzz with news of a gnarly backflip while doing a 360. Pastrana is a former motocross star who has crossed over into other sports–and found success at just about anything he's tried. This almost-impossible trick, though, never had much of a chance, and Pastrana crash-landed. He was too shaken up to try again but, luckily, escaped serious injury. Kyle Loza went on to win the event.

Carmichael goes up and over the bar.

Ricky Steps Up

Ricky Carmichael's nickname is "GOAT"–as in "Greatest of All Time." The supercross and motocross legend tried to defend his step up gold from X Games 14. If you aren't familiar with step up, imagine it as track and field's high jump, only for dirt bikes. Carmichael and Ronnie Renner soared 34 feet, so the two had a jump-off at 35 feet. After Renner failed, Carmichael hit the bar, landing with a thump. Officials awarded dual gold medals.

Gold Is Good

It took Rune Glifberg a long time to reach the winner's circle at the X Games. Once he finally got there in 2008, he decided he liked it so much that he'd come back in 2009! Glifberg's win in 2008 landed him the ninth medal, but only the first gold, of his X Games career. He won again in 2009 with a seemingly effortless performance. Andy MacDonald was second for the second year in a row.

Other notable performances from Summer X Games 15:

✱ Ashley Fiolek won the women's moto X super X competition by overtaking Jessica Patterson on the last lap. Fiolek is deaf, but that hasn't stopped her from becoming a motocross star.

✱ The weekend X Games events at the Home Depot Center near Los Angeles included a moving tribute to Jeremy Lusk, the moto X freestyle gold medalist in 2008. Tragically, Lusk died after crashing during a stunt in an event in San Jose, Costa Rica, in February of 2009.

Glifberg made it back-to-back golds.

2008–09 X GAMES WINNERS

WINTER X GAMES 13
Aspen, Colorado
January 21–25, 2009

Skiing Big Air
Simon Dumont

Skiing Mono SkierX
Tyler Walker

Skiing SkierX (Men)
Stanley Hayer

Skiing SkierX (Women)
Ophelle David

Skiing Slopestyle (Men)
TJ Schiller

Skiing Slopestyle (Women)
Anna Segal

Skiing Superpipe (Men)
Xavier Bertoni

Skiing Superpipe (Women)
Sarah Burke

Snowboard Big Air
Travis Rice

Snowboard Slopestyle (Men)
Shaun White

Snowboard Slopestyle (Women)
Jenny Jones

Snowboard Snowboarder X (Men)
Nate Holland

Snowboard Snowboarder X (Women)
Lindsey Jacobellis

Snowboard Superpipe (Men)
Shaun White

Snowboard Superpipe (Women)
Torah Bright

Snowmobile Freestyle
Joe Parsons

Snowmobile Next Trick
Dane Ferguson

Snowmobile Snocross
Tucker Hibbert

Snowmobile Speed/Style
Joe Parsons

Jenny Jones

SUMMER X GAMES 15
Los Angeles, California
July 29–August 2, 2009

BMX Big Air
Kevin Robinson

BMX Freestyle Street
Garrett Reynolds

BMX Freestyle Park
Scotty Cranmer

BMX Freestyle Vert
Jamie Bestwick

Moto X Best Trick
Kyle Loza

Moto X Best Whip
Todd Potter

Moto X Freestyle
Blake Williams

Moto X Racing (Men)
Josh Hansen

Moto X Racing (Women)
Ashley Fiolek

Moto X Step Up
Ricky Carmichael
Ronnie Renner

Moto X Super Moto
Ivan Lazzarini

Moto X Super X Adaptive
Chris Ridgway

Rally Car Racer
Kenny Brack

Skate Big Air
Jake Brown

Skate Big Air Rail Jam
Danny Way

Skate Street (Men)
Paul Rodriguez

Skate Street (Women)
Marisa Dal Santo

Skate Park
Rune Gilfberg

Skate Park Legends
Christian Hosoi

Skate Vert (Men)
Pierre-Luc Gagnon

Skate Vert (Women)
Lyn-Z Adams Hawkins

Ashley Fiolek

MVP SUPERSTAR!
Guillermo Barros Schelotto led the Columbus Crew to the 2008 MLS title with speed and awesome passing.

2008 CHAMPS, 2009 NEWS

If you see the color yellow on a sign, it usually means "Watch out!" or "Caution!" When Major League Soccer (MLS) teams see bright yellow, they know they have to watch out, too . . . for the powerful Columbus Crew. In 2008, the Crew had the best record in the regular season. Then they stormed through the play-offs and captured their first ever MLS Cup.

In the championship game for the MLS Cup, superstar midfielder Guillermo Barros Schelotto had a Cup-record three assists. But that was nothing new for the player who had also been named the MVP of the entire league for his creative, goal-producing style. The native of Argentina had seven goals and 19 assists during the season and added a record-tying six assists in the play-offs.

The other big news during the 2008 MLS season was English superstar David Beckham joining the Los Angeles Galaxy. After an arrival that seemed more like a rock concert than a sports event, Beckham tried to turn the Galaxy into a good team. While he chipped in with 10 assists and five goals (including one in his first Galaxy home game), he couldn't lead L.A. into the play-offs.

As 2009 began, Beckham wasn't helping them at all . . . he was in Italy. He played during the MLS off-season for AC Milan. Then he decided he'd rather stay there, even when MLS restarted. After lots of discussion and rumors, MLS and AC Milan agreed that Beckham could stay for a while, but that he had to come back to L.A. in July. It was not the sort of support Galaxy fans were hoping for.

Meanwhile, other soccer fans were *loving* their team's success. The Seattle Sounders played their first MLS season in 2009. The team rewarded its loud and boisterous fans with an awesome start. They lost only two of their first nine games and regularly played in front of packed stadiums. The energy from this new team could mean good things in the future, if other cities can follow suit (see page 145).

MAJOR LEAGUE SOCCER

2008 Final Standings

EASTERN CONFERENCE	POINTS
Columbus	57
Chicago	46
New England	43
Kansas City	42
New York	39
D.C. United	37
Toronto	35

WESTERN CONFERENCE	POINTS
Houston	51
Chivas USA	43
Real Salt Lake	40
Colorado	38
FC Dallas	36
Los Angeles	33
San Jose	33

CORNER KICKS

Women's Soccer Returns!

Women's pro soccer returned to the U.S. in 2009 with the debut of, well . . . Women's Pro Soccer (WPS). Seven teams started play in 2009, with two more scheduled to be added in 2010.

Leading the way was Marta (left), the three-time world player of the year. She starred for the Los Angeles Sol. U.S. national team star Abby Wambach was another top WPS player, along with English star Kelly Smith.

The WPS was not the first women's league ever, but earlier attempts at such a league have struggled to succeed. But the WPS plan seems like a strong one. They drew a big crowd for the championship game, in which Sky Blue FC from New Jersey defeated the Sol 1–0.

MLS Gets Bigger

While Seattle and its fans (right) got all the headlines in 2009 with their great start, other cities are looking ahead, too. The Philadelphia Union will join MLS for the 2010 season. A big city with a large population of European and Latin immigrants, Philly should be a hot soccer city.

In the northwest, Seattle will soon have company. In 2011, teams will start play in Portland, Oregon, and Vancouver, Canada. That will make three teams in that part of North America and should create some hot rivalries on the pitch (that's what soccer fans call the field).

European Results

The Red Devils ruled again in England. Manchester United won its 18th English Premier League championship in 2009, tying Liverpool for the most all-time. (The Premier League is the top level of soccer in England, a country that is just nuts about the game . . . which they call "football," of course.) Mighty Man U was led by Portuguese midfielder Cristiano Ronaldo.

However, they could not pull off their hoped-for double championship. In the hotly contested UEFA Champions League final, Barcelona (above) and its superstar Leonel Messi beat Manchester. UEFA is a tournament played by the winners of all the soccer leagues in Europe. Barcelona made the finals with one of the most stunning goals of the year. Needing a goal to advance, they waited until the 92nd minute of the game to score against Chelsea, sending "Barca" fans worldwide into a massive fiesta!

U.S. and the World Cup

With the World Cup looming on the soccer horizon in 2010 (see page 146), the U.S. team (in white at left) has a good shot at being part of the action. A huge upset 2–0 win over mighty Spain (left) in a "friendly" match in June gave them hope. To earn a spot in South Africa in 2010, however, the U.S. must qualify. From June to November, they played a series of games against teams that included Cuba, Guatemala, and Trinidad & Tobago. Only three teams from CONCACAF are guaranteed spots in the 32-team final.

WORLD SUPERSTARS

Who are some of the hottest soccer players on the planet in 2008 and 2009?

KAKA

For a guy who was nearly paralyzed in a swimming accident, Kaka has really bounced back. He has won two World Player of the Year awards and should be a key part of Brazil's 2010 World Cup team. In 2009, Real Madrid paid a then-record $92 million to have him join their team!

Kaka aims for a goal—and a Cup—for Brazil.

Lionel MESSI

Small, fast, smart, Messi is the perfect passing superstar . . . but he's also brave enough to take the ball in against bigger defenders. Messi plays for Barcelona and his pass led to the goal that sent them to the UEFA Cup final in 2009. He'll be a star for Argentina in World Cup 2010.

Cristiano RONALDO

In the toughest league on the planet, Ronaldo was the biggest star. He led Manchester United with 42 goals in 49 games. In 2010, though, he joined Kaka at Real Madrid for a stunning $131 million!

Other names to watch in 2010:

Didier DROGBA: One of the world's best scorers, will his country (Ivory Coast) even be in the World Cup?

Stephen GERRARD: Can the player they call the "engine" of the beloved England team carry them to the top?

RONALDHINO: Will the Brazilian come back from a thigh injury to reclaim his spot as the world's best?

"I never think about the play or visualize anything. I do what comes to me at that moment. Instinct. It has always been that way."

— LIONEL MESSI

WORLD CUP 2010

In December 2009, the 32 teams that will take part in the World Cup finals will be organized into eight groups of four teams each. Those teams will then practice and train for six months before heading south . . . waaaayyy south, to take part in the World Cup.

South Africa will be the first African nation to host this quadrennial soccer extravaganza. Beginning on June 11, nine South African cities will host matches that will be watched by billions around the world. The World Cup gets more attention worldwide than any other sporting event (that's right, we think it's bigger than the Olympics!).

Italy (captain Fabio Cannavaro, right) should be back to defend its 2006 title, while South Africa is guaranteed a spot as the host country. Look for soccer nations like Brazil, Spain, and Germany to send solid teams to the finals. However, even those top countries have to go through a long qualifying process that will last until November. (Check out what the United States has to deal with on page 145).

THE CRYSTAL SOCCER BALL

We've put on our fortune-teller's hat and peered into the amazing crystal soccer ball, and we have the answer you need. Here is the country we think will come home with the World Cup trophy (check back in July to see if we were right):

SPAIN

STAT STUFF

MAJOR LEAGUE SOCCER CHAMPIONS

Year	Champion
2008	Columbus Crew
2007	Houston Dynamo
2006	Houston Dynamo
2005	Los Angeles Galaxy
2004	D.C. United
2003	San Jose Earthquakes
2002	Los Angeles Galaxy
2001	San Jose Earthquakes
2000	Kansas City Wizards
1999	D.C. United
1998	Chicago Fire
1997	D.C. United
1996	D.C. United

World Cup Scoring Leaders

MEN

GOALS	PLAYER, COUNTRY
15	Ronaldo, Brazil
14	Gerd Müller, West Germany
13	Just Fontaine, France
12	Pelé, Brazil
11	Jürgen Klinsmann, Germany
11	Sandor Kocsis, Hungary

WOMEN

GOALS	PLAYER, COUNTRY
14	Birgit Prinz, Germany
12	Michelle Akers, United States
11	Sun Wen, China
11	Bettina Wiegmann, Germany

WORLD CUP RESULTS

YEAR	WINNER	RUNNER-UP
2006	**Italy**	France
2002	**Brazil**	Germany
1998	**France**	Brazil
1994	**Brazil**	Italy
1990	**West Germany**	Argentina
1986	**Argentina**	West Germany
1982	**Italy**	West Germany
1978	**Argentina**	Netherlands
1974	**West Germany**	Netherlands
1970	**Brazil**	Italy
1966	**England**	West Germany
1962	**Brazil**	Czechoslovakia
1958	**Brazil**	Sweden
1954	**West Germany**	Hungary
1950	**Uruguay**	Brazil
1938	**Italy**	Hungary
1934	**Italy**	Czechoslovakia
1930	**Uruguay**	Argentina

Note: The World Cup was canceled in 1942 and 1946 due to World War II.

TIGER'S BACK!

Golf was quiet for most of the second half of 2008 and the first half of 2009. Of course, golf is normally a quiet sport; fans are expected to remain silent while players are on the course. However, this was another kind of quiet. This quiet was the absence of a roar . . . the roar of a Tiger. But when the silence was broken, the roar was enormous!

Tiger Woods, the world's greatest golfer, underwent knee surgery in June and was out of competition for eight months. While Tiger was away, Padraig Harrington and others took advantage. The Irish golfer earned his second straight PGA Championship after having also captured the 2008 British Open.

Vijay Singh also enjoyed the absence of Tiger. Vijay earned enough points after only three of the four FedEx Cup events to win the trophy . . . and the $10 million first prize! Vijay has been among the world's best for many years, but not having Tiger in the field made it possible for him to capture the big prize.

However, as 2009 began, every golf fan was just counting the days until Tiger returned. He played a few events early and then leaped back into the spotlight in March. Trailing by six shots entering the final round of the Bay Hill Classic, Woods put on another stunning display of golf. He caught and then tied Sean O'Hair. Then Tiger buried a 15-foot birdie putt on the final hole to set off another fist-pumping celebration.

In May 2009, another top golfer headed for the sidelines. Phil Mickelson left to help his wife, who was battling breast cancer. The absences of superstars such as Tiger and Phil opened the door for some young golfers to make their marks on the PGA Tour (see box on page 153). The door stayed open at the U.S. Open in June, when 29-year-old Lucas Glover won his first major championship. Veteran Stewart Cink (British Open) and youngster Y. E. Yang (who stared down Tiger in the final round of the PGA Championship) also won their first majors.

Tiger's back on the prowl for good, but maybe now he'll have some company in the hunt for golf's biggest trophies.

2009 MAJOR CHAMPIONSHIP WINNERS

THE MASTERS
Angel Cabrera

THE U.S. OPEN
Lucas Glover

THE BRITISH OPEN
Stewart Cink

THE PGA CHAMPIONSHIP
Y. E. Yang

GOLF

I'M BAAAACK!
Red fashion on Sunday is a Tiger tradition. So is winning in dramatic fashion. Tiger exults here after a clutch putt gave him a come-from-behind win shortly after coming back from serious knee surgery.

WE WON THE CUP!

Anthony Kim's golf club got put to better use as he waved the flag at the Ryder Cup.

The United States captured the Ryder Cup for the first time since 1999! (Non-golf fans: See inset for what the Ryder Cup is!) Their five-point victory over the European squad was the biggest margin since 1981!

And they did it all . . . without Tiger Woods. Captain Paul Azinger masterfully mixed some veterans with a host of young talent to turn the three-day event into stars and stripes "fore"-ever.

The key matches on the final day pitted American Ryder rookie Anthony Kim against Spanish star Sergio Garcia, whom he defeated. Fellow rookies J. B. Holmes and Boo Weekley also won Sunday singles matches to help the U.S. clinch the Cup.

For golfers who usually only play alone, being on this team always means a lot. Winning makes it even more special.

"I got chills up my spine the whole day today, and I'm loving every minute of it," said Kim when it was all over.

THE RYDER CUP Held every two years, this event pits a team of 12 American golfers against a squad of 12 Europeans. Until 1979, the Ryder Cup was between Great Britain and America only, but it expanded after the U.S. won every tournament from 1936 to 1977 and it got too boring. Since its first win in 1985, Europe holds an 8–4 lead. Why Ryder? British businessman Samuel Ryder donated the trophy in 1927.

Another Cup

In October 2009, captains Fred Couples (U.S.) and Greg Norman (International) lead their teams into another golfing championship. The Presidents' Cup matches American golfers against golfers from outside Europe.

Viva Angel!

At the Masters in April 2009, Angel Cabrera became the first golfer from Argentina to win this important event. Cabrera fought off Chad Campbell and Kenny Perry and won the green jacket on the second play-off hole, following a 72-hole tie. In another first, Korean-born Y. E. Yang became the first Asian golfer to win a major when he captured the PGA Championship.

UP NEXT ON THE TEE

Golfers to watch in 2010 and beyond:

ZACH JOHNSON: The 2007 Master championship signaled the start of a fine career, and two wins in early 2009 showed that Johnson was here to stay. A smooth swinger, Johnson has a calm beyond his youth and should be among the leaders for many years.

ANTHONY KIM: While Zach is laid-back, Kim is much more visible. His enthusiastic play, his huge belt buckles, and his championship game mark him as a player to watch.

WEBB SIMPSON: A former college star, Webb won a tournament to join the PGA Tour. In his first few months, he was near the top of several tournaments. Here's a vote that he'll end up on top before too long.

THE LADIES' TEES

Another trophy for superstar Lorena.

The 2008 LPGA season was all about one golfer: Lorena Ochoa of Mexico. She won her third straight Player of the Year award, while racking up seven event wins . . . including four in a row! She played in 22 events and was in the top five in 13. She also added another major title, the Kraft Nabisco Championship.

Ochoa, from Mexico, has become the female Tiger Woods, expected to win often and often coming through. She added two more wins in the first half of 2009 to keep her star shining.

Who can challenge Ochoa in 2009 and beyond? How about Yani Tseng, a superstar in the making. She finished second in five events and won the LPGA Championship for her first major. Paula Creamer had another fine season in 2008 with seven top-five finishes. With superstar Annika Sorenstam moving on (see box below), the LPGA is Ochoa's. . . . Watch out, Tiger!

GOOD-BYE, ANNIKA

Was she the greatest female golfer ever? There are some experts who would say "Jah!" Of course, that would mean they are from her native Sweden, but they'd still be right. Annika Sorenstam retired at the end of the 2008 season. Among her many accomplishments, she won 72 LPGA events, 10 of them Majors, and was the Player of the Year eight times! She was a dominant force in her sport for 15 years, but only 38 when she retired. She was also the first woman in 58 years to hit the links with the boys in a PGA Tour event.

CHIP SHOTS

Gee. Surprise. Wow.

Another amazing comeback by golf's greatest player. Tiger Woods trailed by four strokes entering the final round of the Memorial Tournament in June 2009. As he has done so many times, he came back on the final Sunday. The victory was his fourth at the Memorial in his amazing career.

Pink Is In!

John Daly wore pink pants during a tournament in June. He was cheered, however, for his unusual fashion choice, because he was supporting Amy Mickelson, wife of star player Phil Mickelson. She was diagnosed with cancer in May and Phil left the Tour to be with her. Thousands contacted Mickelson to offer their support, and Daly's pants were just the most visible backslap. ▼

Golf Idol ▸▸

Pop star and golf nut Justin Timberlake hosted a PGA Tour event, encouraging young fans to play the sport . . . when they're not dancing to his music.

Nice Shot!

Annika Sorenstam's final shot at a U.S. Open was a stunning 200-yard six iron for an eagle. Nice way to go out!

Turning Boos into Yeas!

One of the surprise stars of the Ryder Cup (page 152) was long-hitting, fun-loving Boo Weekley. The guy who once complained that he couldn't get good fried chicken in Scotland said he thought his Ryder Cup tuxedo would feel like a straitjacket. His down-home charm kept his teammates and fans laughing all the way to the championship.

Shorts Shot

When his ball landed in the mud in the bottom of a pond, Henrik Stenson had a chance to hit it out. But he didn't want to get his clothes messy. So he took off his golf shoes and socks . . . and his pants . . . and waded in to hit the ball out. Don't worry, he was wearing shorts, but it was still a pretty odd sight!

THE MAJORS

In golf, some tournaments are known as the Majors. They're the four most important events of the year on either the men's or women's pro tours. Tiger Woods is rapidly moving up the ranks in career wins in Majors. On the women's side, Annika Sorenstam has the most among recent golfers.

MEN'S

GOLFER	MASTERS	U.S. OPEN	BRITISH OPEN	PGA CHAMP.	TOTAL
Jack **NICKLAUS**	6	4	3	5	**18**
Tiger **WOODS**	4	3	3	4	**14**
Walter **HAGEN**	0	2	4	5	**11**
Ben **HOGAN**	2	4	1	2	**9**
Gary **PLAYER**	3	1	3	2	**9**
Tom **WATSON**	2	1	5	0	**8**
Arnold **PALMER**	4	1	2	0	**7**
Gene **SARAZEN**	1	2	1	3	**7**
Sam **SNEAD**	3	0	1	3	**7**
Harry **VARDON**	0	1	6	0	**7**

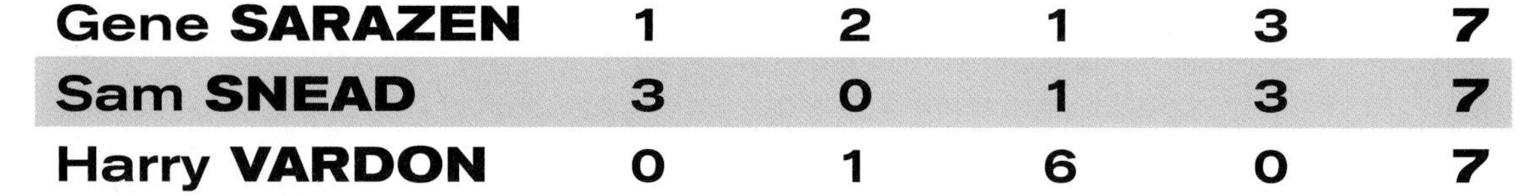

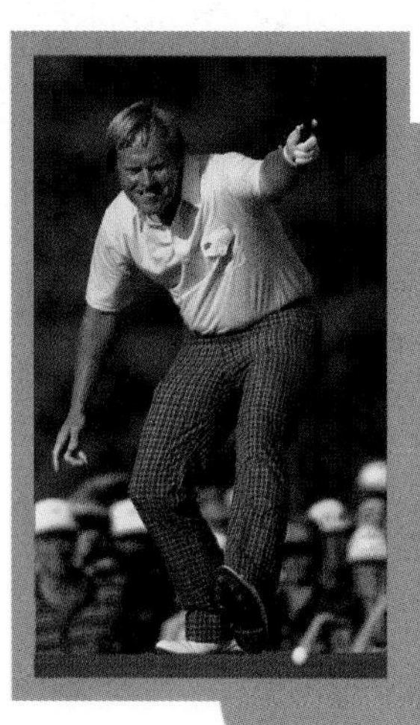

THE GOLDEN BEAR

Fans today marvel at the accomplishments of Tiger Woods. They call him "the best ever" and "something we've never seen before." Um, not so fast. There's still a guy out there ahead of Tiger in Major titles. Jack Nicklaus, known as "The Golden Bear" for his blond hair and early-career girth, was a star in the 1960s and 1970s. Nicklaus combined a long game with superclutch putting to win his record 18 majors. His six Masters green jackets remains an all-time best, too. He's also one of the five men who have won each of the four Majors. Until Tiger hits 19, we'll keep Jack at the top of our list.

WOMEN'S

GOLFER	LPGA	USO	BO	NAB	MAUR	TH	WES	TOTAL
Patty **BERG**	0	1	x	x	x	7	7	15
Mickey **WRIGHT**	4	4	x	x	x	2	3	13
Louise **SUGGS**	1	2	x	x	x	4	4	11
Babe **ZAHARIAS**	x	3	x	x	x	3	4	10
Annika **SORENSTAM**	3	3	1	3	x	x	x	10
Betsy **RAWLS**	2	4	x	x	x	x	2	8
Karrie **WEBB**	1	2	1	2	1	x	x	7
Juli **INKSTER**	2	2	x	2	1	x	x	7

KEY: LPGA = LPGA Championship, USO = U.S. Open, BO = British Open, NAB = Nabisco Championship, MAUR = Du Maurier (1979–2000), TH = Titleholders (1937–1972), WES = Western Open (1937–1967)

PGA TOUR CAREER EARNINGS

1.	Tiger Woods	$85,601,189
2.	Vijay Singh	$61,513,603
3.	Phil Mickelson	$53,761,536
4.	Jim Furyk	$40,957,429
5.	Davis Love III	$38,546,069
6.	Ernie Els	$34,612,511
7.	David Toms	$30,243,380
8.	Kenny Perry	$28,973,147
9.	Justin Leonard	$28,363,528
10.	Stewart Cink	$26,109,470

LPGA TOUR CAREER EARNINGS

1.	Annika Sorenstam	$22,573,192
2.	Karrie Webb	$14,688,555
3.	Lorena Ochoa	$13,890,414
4.	Juli Inkster	$12,569,213
5.	Se Ri Pak	$10,407,768

Patty Berg

While today's female golf fans recognize names like Sorenstam, Lopez, or Inkster, and sports history fans know about Zaharias, the name at the top of the above list is not as well known. Patty Berg played her best golf in the 1950s. She was one of the founding members of the LPGA and was its first president. In the early ladies' pro game, she was one of the best, winning 44 pro titles through 1962. In 1967, she was one of the first members of the LPGA Hall of Fame. A great teacher, Berg said that she had taught more than 500,000 people to play.

TENNIS

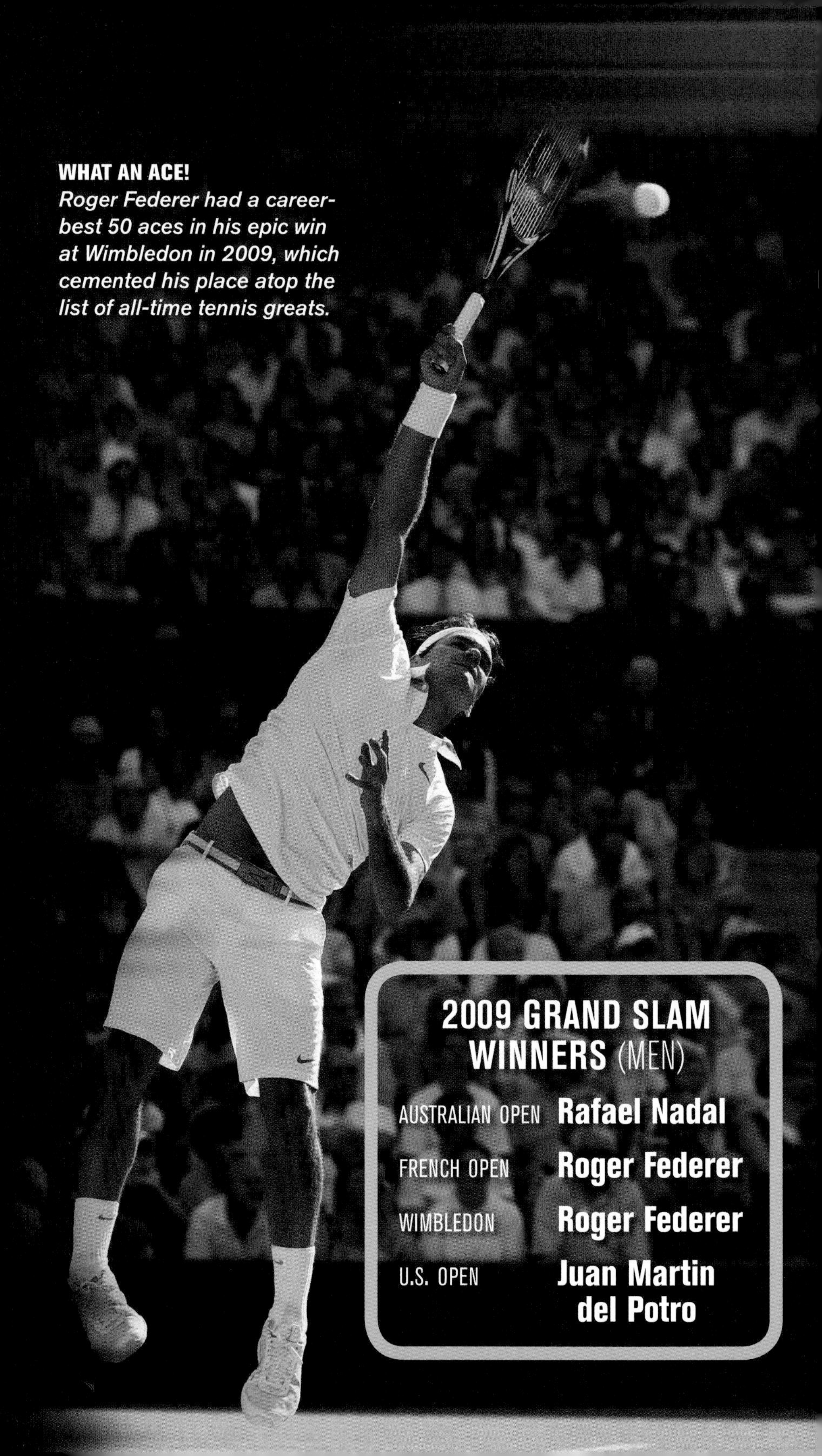

WHAT AN ACE!
Roger Federer had a career-best 50 aces in his epic win at Wimbledon in 2009, which cemented his place atop the list of all-time tennis greats.

2009 GRAND SLAM WINNERS (MEN)

AUSTRALIAN OPEN	**Rafael Nadal**
FRENCH OPEN	**Roger Federer**
WIMBLEDON	**Roger Federer**
U.S. OPEN	**Juan Martin del Potro**

LOVE 15!

You can say you saw him at his best. You can proudly boast that you got to see Roger Federer win more Grand Slam tennis titles than any other male player. And you can say that you saw him do it with calm, grace, and a surprising amount of toughness.

In the longest final match in the long history of Wimbledon (they've been playing this tournament near London since 1887!), Federer beat American Andy Roddick (see box) to win his 6th title there . . . and his 15th Grand Slam title. That moved him past Pete Sampras to become the all-time leader in championships in the four key tennis titles (see chart on page 162).

In tennis, you have to win each set by two games. And at Wimbledon, they don't use tiebreakers in the final set. That means the two men played on and on . . . and on! . . . until one had gained a two-game margin. The final set went (are you ready for this?) 30 games! A normal set might have 8 or 10 or 12 games. Federer finally prevailed 16–14. The match set a record for most games in any Grand Slam final (77) and was also the longest fifth set ever. Until 2009, both of those records had held since 1927!

Federer's final run to the record actually began the previous fall in New York City. After he lost at Wimbledon in 2008–in yet another amazing five-set masterpiece–to Spanish superstar Rafael Nadal, some tennis fans wondered if the great Swiss star was fading. Federer rallied in the fall, however, to win his fifth straight U.S. Open. That put him one short of Sampras's record. Then Federer lost to Nadal at the 2009 Australian Open, too. At the French Open, however, Federer got his revenge on four-time French winner Nadal, winning Grand Slam title No. 14 after Nadal was upset by Robin Soderling earlier in the tourney. Federer wasn't so lucky at the end of the year: At the U.S. Open in September, he was upset in the final by Juan Martin del Potro of Argentina. Federer's hunt for No. 16 will continue in 2010!

ANYTHING BUT A LOSER

Andy Roddick hung his head as he sat in a chair beside Wimbledon's Centre Court. He shouldn't have. His grit and strength and courage in his epic battle with Federer earned him as much applause as the winner got. Roddick had been disappointed before at Wimbledon. He has lost three finals to Federer, along with a final-match loss to the Swiss champ at the 2006 U.S. Open.

America's best male tennis player has just one Grand Slam title on his record, the 2003 U.S. Open. However, his positive, let's-get-it-next-time approach to all his near misses makes him a winner in our book.

THE SISTER ACT CONTINUES

Serena (left) won at Wimbledon in '09, but Venus is a five-time champ.

The Williams sisters have been the story in women's tennis since they first started winning major tournaments in the late 1990s. Their domination of the Grand Slam events, and their battles with each other at times, have made them living tennis legends.

Their run continued in 2009, as Serena captured another French Open title and then defeated her sister to earn her third Wimbledon championship. She's still two short of Venus's amazing five Wimbledon titles, however, so big sis has that to brag about!

The pair's success story has defined women's tennis in the past decade. Venus turned pro when she was only 14 and emerged on the world stage as a runner-up at the 1997 U.S. Open. Two years later, Serena upstaged her older sister by winning Wimbledon.

In 2000, they teamed up to win a gold medal in doubles at the Summer Olympics. It's been a Williams decade ever since, with the duo earning a stunning 18 Grand Slam titles between them. For various periods one of them has been ranked number one in the world, and on several occasions, they've been ranked one-two.

In an era in which few other female Americans, if any, have even sniffed the top of the rankings, the Williamses have been a dominant sister act.

2009 Grand Slam Winners
(WOMEN)

AUSTRALIAN OPEN	**Serena Williams**
FRENCH OPEN	**Svetlana Kuznetsova**
WIMBLEDON	**Serena Williams**
U.S. OPEN	**Kim Clijsters**

OTHER BIG MOMENTS FROM 2009

- Down Goes Nadal I: Robin Soderling of Switzerland was a surprise winner over clay-court master Rafael Nadal in the French Open. That opened the door for Federer to win in France.
- Down Goes Nadal II: A knee injury forced Nadal to skip the Wimbledon tournament. Will he be able to bounce back from his time off?
- To Grunt or Not to Grunt: Grumblings about grunting filled the air before Wimbledon. Officials said that players who make a loud grunt or yell as they hit big shots were spoiling the moment. (Loudest grunter? Maria Sharapova at 101 decibels, or almost as loud as a lion's roar.) No one was penalized, but look for this "noisy" discussion to continue.

FROM RUSSIA IN TENNIS SHOES

Other than the Williams sisters, almost a country by themselves, the top tennis nation for female players is Russia. Through the middle of 2009, five of the top ten women in the world hailed from Russia. Two others are from Eastern European countries: Belarus and Serbia.

Dinara Safina (below) is one of the best Russian players. She was the women's player of the year in 2008. She has 11 singles titles, but is still working on her first Grand Slam victory. In the meantime, she's being pushed by countrywomen such as Elena Dementieva and Svetlana Kuznetsova. Are there more great tennis players coming from those often-snowy lands? The answer is probably "Da!"

STAT STUFF

ALL-TIME GRAND SLAM CHAMPIONSHIPS (MEN)

	AUS. OPEN	FRENCH OPEN	WIMBLEDON	U.S. OPEN	TOTAL
Roger **FEDERER**	3	1	6	5	**15**
Pete **SAMPRAS**	2	0	7	5	**14**
Roy **EMERSON**	6	2	2	2	**12**
Bjorn **BORG**	0	6	5	0	**11**
Rod **LAVER**	3	2	4	2	**11**
Bill **TILDEN**	0	0	3	7	**10**
Jimmy **CONNORS**	1	0	2	5	**8**
Ivan **LENDL**	2	3	0	3	**8**
Fred **PERRY**	1	1	3	3	**8**
Ken **ROSEWALL**	4	2	0	2	**8**
Andre **AGASSI**	4	1	1	2	**8**

THE FORMER CHAMP

American Pete Sampras cheered when Roger Federer won Wimbledon in 2009, but he was also clapping for the end of his own time on top. Sampras dominated men's tennis in the 1990s, using his big serve and solid game to rack up seven Wimbledon titles. He also won five U.S. Opens.

ALL-TIME GRAND SLAM CHAMPIONSHIPS (WOMEN)

	AUS.	FRENCH	WIMBLEDON	U.S.	TOTAL
Margaret Smith **COURT**	11	5	3	5	**24**
Steffi **GRAF**	4	6	7	5	**22**
Helen Wills **MOODY**	0	4	8	7	**19**
Chris **EVERT**	2	7	3	6	**18**
Martina **NAVRATILOVA**	3	2	9	4	**18**
Billie Jean **KING**	1	1	6	4	**12**
Serena **WILLIAMS**	3	2	3	3	**11**
Maureen **CONNOLLY**	1	2	3	3	**9**
Monica **SELES**	4	3	0	2	**9**
Suzanne **LENGLEN**	0	2*	6	0	**8**
Molla Bjurstedt **MALLORY**	0	0	0	8	**8**

*Also won four French titles before 1925; in those years, the tournament was open only to French nationals.

The All-Time Champ

She won when she was just Margaret Smith. Then she got married, added a name appropriate for tennis, and became Margaret Smith Court. And she kept winning. Throughout the 1960s and early 1970s, she dominated women's tennis, winning every major over and over.

The Australian native was a big player with a big game. She overpowered opponents with her serve, or used her strength to boom shots from the baseline. In 1970, she rolled it all together, becoming only the second player ever to win the Grand Slam itself: all four major titles in one calendar year. Her final career total of 24 Grand Slams remains the best ever.

OTHER SPORTS

WINTER WINNER!

Lindsey Vonn became the most successful female skier in American history in 2009, winning her second World Cup overall title. Vonn has her ski tips pointed toward the 2010 Winter Olympic Games, scheduled for February in Vancouver, Canada. Read more about Lindsey and the stars of some other cool sports in this info-packed chapter.